Punished!

A
Black Velvet Seductions
Anthology

Richard Savage

Nadia Nautalia

Starla Kaye

www.blackvelvetseductions.com

ISBN 978-1-936556-51-9

Published 2014
Printed by Black Velvet Seductions Publishing
Company in the United States of America

Visit us at:
www.blackvelvetseductions.com

Table of Contents

Richard Savage

In the Driving Seat

Barbara gritted her teeth, her father had been right,

Alan was a pig! The indignity! How dare he do this! She loved shopping, but he always spoiled it by bitching about every cent she spent. God she hated this petty debate every time she spent a dime on herself. Couldn't he just enjoy the fact that she looked good?

His grim funeral director's face stared back at her over the breakfast table. Barbara tried to coax him out of his foul mood with what she hoped was one of her winning smiles. Alan sat there, seemingly unmoved by either her attempts to lighten the mood, or the aromas of coffee that mingled with the sweet pungent smell of grilled bacon, filling the kitchen.

He had the credit card bill open, lying accusingly in front of him on the table. His features looked as if they had been carved from a slab of granite. His eyes were cold and hard, as though he was about to announce some great natural catastrophe had occurred. This happened every damn time the credit card bill arrived and it made her feel sick to her stomach!

She found his rigid control over the finances unsettling, as if nothing in her life was really certain or stable. She had always found shopping a comfort, but Alan had destroyed the pleasure in that, making her feel guilty, with his constant scrutiny of bank statements.

She longed for the time in their early marriage when he had been lighter, before his constant nagging about money, when he had treated her like a princess to be pampered and spoiled. In an attempt to rekindle those early feelings, she tried to summon up a smile but saw not a glimmer of his mood melting.

A trickle of alarm slid through her, refusing to be squelched. He did seem more angry than usual this morning. There was something in his manner, coldness, and distance that hadn't been there before.

She watched as his eyes narrowed and his fork clattered to the plate. She shivered a little and moved in her seat as she felt a wave of cold wash over her.

Like a volcano, Alan erupted, "You have to be fucking kidding? This is a credit card statement?"

She watched as his cheeks flushed and his nostrils flared. She heard the rush of air over his teeth. He was barely containing his rage. His sudden ferocity shocked her. He had gotten angry before, but he had never exploded quite like this.

She felt lost, alone, empty in the face of Alan's explosive anger, and it frightened her.

"This is ours? Right?" He shook the piece of paper. "I was just wondering if I had opened the statement for the third world debt by mistake."

Barbara felt herself smile, involuntarily. She had always loved his sense of humor, but she hated it when he used it sarcastically. It was like having something she loved used against her as a weapon. Her teeth squeezed her lower lip, as she tried to suppress the deep sadness that filled her, threatening to overwhelm her. She'd felt herself succumbing to this familiar feeling of sadness and isolation as Alan had become stingier and stingier.

As she sat before him she felt her anger rising as she thought of him goading her. She found it frustrating, as there really was no reply to his sarcastic humor.

"Well? The shoes. Are they solid gold? Or what?"

"What the hell, do you know of style?"

"I know how fucking much it costs." She saw the muscles in his jaw go tight.

Alan felt the anger bubble inside him like the agitated fermenting of an angry sea. His anger was a boiling churning cauldron of bile, souring the taste in his mouth, as it frothed climbing ever higher on the inside of his mind. He saw red and boiled over. What the fuck was he to do with her?

His mind turned the events over, his patience at an end. It drove him crazy, that with Barbara it was all material things.

He knew her father had always given gifts to compensate for his lack of time with her. *Gifts—things instead of time.* He sighed. He could easily understand why Barbara equated gifts with love and why she believed that money could buy happiness but he hated that outlook.

The situation was desperate and as he sat there, despair clouding his thoughts his thoughts turned to the article he'd read in a magazine while waiting for a haircut.

The article had been about domestic discipline. The writer of the article had claimed that the introduction of spanking had saved his marriage.

He had read about spanking in adult magazines before and he found the whole idea arousing, but he had never considered it in terms of repairing his relationship with Barbara.

He rolled his shoulders. Maybe spanking would be the magic bullet that would save their marriage.

Her words from another fight over money came flooding back into his head, "Maybe I could just ask daddy for my allowance back, or maybe he could give you a raise."

He felt a moment of calm, that silent spell before the thunderclap. His fists came together in front of him scrunching the flimsy paper into a ball. "I hold the purse strings in this house! Is that clearly understood?"

"Yes Sir," her voice was small, that of a lost little girl, standing at the headmaster's desk.

She looked so innocent, her head cast down, her eyes looking up at him. There was the expression of a little girl sorry for doing wrong and it tugged at him making him want to wrap her up in his arms and tell her it would be okay, but he'd done that many times before. The other part of him was intensely irritated by her blatant attempt to manipulate him.

He knew this meek and mild stance was all a part of the game. She wanted to slip from the hook, as he had let her in the past. Yet he knew that he could not go on like this. This time he had to be strong, one way or another, this had to stop. A line had to be drawn.

"You have two choices. Either we go back to the shop and I stand there while you tell the manager that $1500 is a ridiculous price for a pair of shoes and your husband won't allow you to spend that kind of money or..."

Barbara smirked and half giggled at the absurdity of her trying to do that. The humiliation would be unbearable. She had shopped at that particular store since she had been old enough to buy her own shoes. The staff knew her. Returning the shoes like that was *not* an option

Alan's jaw tightened "You think this is funny?"

She watched as he folded his arms, a wall of defiant muscle before her.

"Your alternative is to submit to a spanking."

She felt her jaw slacken. She could not believe what she was hearing. He had to be kidding. She looked at him incredulously.

The wooden dining chair slid back on the kitchen's quarry tiled floor and he stood. She felt intimidated by his sheer physical presence as he drew himself to his full height, shoulders back, shirt tight across his chest.

Spanking? Surely he was not serious. Her stomach churned, this was crazy. She felt her hackles rising, as the thought of him spanking her filled her mind.

"This is a joke right? You *are* kidding?" She folded her arms indignantly across her chest.

He put his hands in his pockets, and rocked back on his heels. "I *am* going spank you," he said simply, in a matter of fact voice, as if he was announcing that it was time for supper.

He took a step toward her.

"You *are* the one that has to be kidding now! I have not been spanked since I was four."

She felt dwarfed by him and took a step backwards. It was as if the walls were closing in, her field of vision narrowing. She felt small and insignificant, in the shadow of his massive frame.

"If your father had taken you firmly in hand earlier, this would not be necessary now."

She watched the twitch in his cheek and was mesmerized by his furrowed brow. He was not messing about, and she knew her attitude was making him even more angry, but she didn't care. Her own blood was boiling. How *bloody* dare he talk to her like this? The thought of being physically punished for buying shoes was absurd. There was no way she was going to submit to this.

Barbara stood. She felt her jaw clench.

She watched as his grimace slowly transformed to a grin of pearly white teeth that left her feeling a bit like Little Red Riding Hood confronted by the wolf for the first time. His smile was disconcerting. It made her feel as if he knew something that she did not.

He stood there as immoveable as Mount Rushmore.

He flexed his shoulders. "So you are defying me?" His eyebrows rose in an impressive arch.

She said nothing but didn't break eye contact. The turmoil inside her grew. She wanted to fight him, yet she knew she didn't have the strength. She wanted to hit him and at the same time she wanted to cry and run for sanctuary. A warm flush hit her face while a cold tingle ran down her spine radiating to pins and needles in her fingers.

He folded his arms across his barrel like chest, his back ramrod straight, unyielding. "I did think of a third option, maybe it would suit you better."

He paused and Barbara racked her brain, searching for options of her own. There must be something. Maybe he would settle for a blowjob. The smile on his face sure hinted at that. She was sure it would pacify him for a while. She returned his smile, happy to have been let off the hook. She began to relax a little more thinking the storm was about to pass. A bullet dodged.

The expression on his face didn't change. "I could send you home to daddy. I am sure he would be delighted to have his little girl back.

Her heart sank into a bottomless pit of despair. Christ no! After all the fights with her father there was no way she could ever go back there to live.

"I'm sure he'd be delighted to be proved right. I'm sure he would be overjoyed to see you could not hack it in the real world." His words were cruel, yet she felt the truth in them.

A cold fear welled up inside her. She fidgeted with the hem of her skirt unsure what to say, searching for the words. A lump caught in her throat, she could not believe he was serious. He was talking about divorce, over shoes.

A flash of anger tingled through her fingers and she felt a warm flush across her cheek.

She tried to keep her composure. Maybe a little break would give him time to cool down and reconsider. Maybe it would make him a bit more reasonable.

"Give me the car keys." She spat the words like venom, fists clenched, expensive manicured nails pressing into her palms. A wave of cold washed over her again.

Alan threw his head back and laughed, "Not a chance! You leave here with what you brought to this house, a jewelry box, if you can carry it, and a shitty attitude. I suppose you might as well take these shoes. Better still walk home in them, I bet you won't get five yards."

She felt the finality of his words clear through her soul. She wiped her moistened palms on the soft fabric of her skirt. Would he seriously throw away their marriage for this?

She felt a pain in her chest. How could she have pushed him this far?

In an epiphany, she saw how trivial possessions were when weighed against her love for Alan. With this new insight glittering in her mind, she knew with clarity that she could not lose him; she would do anything to keep that from happening. He was her life, her bedrock and she could not see a world without him in it.

She felt her heart pounding in her chest as she looked up at him, looking for anything that would tell her she'd misunderstood, that he still loved her. There was nothing on his face that gave her the reassurance she so desperately needed.

The scenes of their marriage flashed through her mind, like snippets from a movie, each one bringing her closer to the dreadful, predictable end.

She saw by his chiseled, marble face, that he was not going to budge an inch. He was a man on the edge and she had pushed him there. She flinched, as a wave of guilt washed over her. She had really not meant to go this far. What she wanted above all else, was for him to make her his princess again. She felt herself wither, deflating like a balloon.

How could she leave? While her father never bitched about her spending he never gave her the feeling of being loved, protected, safe, nurtured, the way Alan had in their early marriage, before they had started to fight about how much money she spent. In walking away from Alan, she would walk away from everything she wanted.

She didn't want to leave and there was no way she could go back to the shop and return the shoes. She had run out of options. Her heart sank. The spanking was inevitable.

"God please Alan, let's not do this." A tone of pleading entered her voice. Her mind was an emotional briar patch, a tangle of mixed emotions. "Can't we just make up? I promise not to do this again."

Alan smirked, slowly shaking his head, "I remember you saying that last time. Oh yes, and the time before." He folded his arms across his chest.

"It will be different this time, I promise."

"Barbara, we have been here before." Alan looked at her, his gaze met hers, pinning her, making her feel like a moth trapped in the glare of a bright light.

"I am not doing this to be a horrible bastard." His fingertips stroked her cheek. "I love you. I really do want you to be happy. I just want you to be content with what we have."

She turned her head to the side, "And you think spanking me will make me content?" she asked, not understanding how a spanking would make her happy.

"Frankly, yes I do. You lack discipline and respect."

Not really having a reply for him she looked at the floor, the hollow void of shame enveloped her. Her head lowered in contemplation as she bowed to the inevitable.

"I take it that you are staying to face the music?" His expression was resolute. His tone was not of satisfaction. In fact, he seemed to be doing this reluctantly, rather than taking pleasure in it.

Maybe he *was* doing it for her own good.

She was aware of her own breathing, conscious the regular beat of her heart, as she remained silent looking at her feet. She felt a little sick, and her throat ached with the pent up need to cry, but no tears came.

His words came abruptly, cold and sharp, precise; his voice louder than it had been before. "Do you submit to corporal punishment?"

The sudden raising of tension, his unexpectedly harsh tone caught her off guard. She realized with horror that her bladder had let her down and she had wet herself. She closed her eyes in shame even though she knew the small leak remained her private shame.

"Yes." Her voice sounded small and dejected even to her own ears.

"You will address me as Sir during punishment." His voice was stern, as if he was talking to a member of his crew rather than his wife and it made her feel worthless and hollow.

"Yes Sir." She felt degraded and dirty, her wet panties making her feel even more childlike and unworthy of her husband.

"Strip, here in front of me please." His words were cool and matter-of-fact.

The simplicity of his words stunned her. There was a surreal quality, as if it was a dream and any moment she would wake up and find herself looking at her breakfast. But the stark reality was staring her in the face. Looking to his eyes, she saw Alan's jaw tighten and his brow furrow deeply. She wanted to comply, but she felt as if the wind had been taken from her sails. A million questions raced through her mind. How, in God's name, had it come to this? How could shopping have brought her to the edge of divorce?

"I want you to strip." His cold, clipped words dragged her from her own thoughts.

"Yes Sir." She felt a lump in her throat, felt the tears welling up, but fought them back. She caught the inside of her lip between her teeth. The sharpness kept her focused on what she had to do.

Her gaze climbed up his chest to meet his gaze, as she slipped off one shoe and then the other. They clattered noisily, as they fell onto the quarry-stone kitchen floor. Her gaze dropped as manicured fingernails slowly undid the buttons of her blouse. She looked up hoping to see some approval in his eyes, some softening, but she was disappointed to see only his steely resolve.

She shrugged off the blouse and laid it on the kitchen chair. She fought back the lump in her throat. She did not want him to see how lost she felt. She wanted to maintain at least that much dignity.

"Very nice." His words were simple but she thought she could hear a little of the ice melting.

Her teeth gripped her lip a little harder, tightening her resolve. She shivered and thumbed the bra strap from her shoulder as she reached around to release the clasp. She sensed his eyes burning into her naked flesh as she stood there feeling vulnerable and exposed. She lifted her arms to cover her breasts.

"I want to see you." His words sounded a little softer, which lifted her spirits a little.

Barbara looked up again, his face had softened slightly. His brow was less menacing and there was a hint of a smile, only a hint, but it made him look more approachable. She found it strangely arousing, almost as if she were an exotic dancer performing for a single client. She liked that he was giving her his full attention; it was almost like regaining a little dignity.

There was something erotic about the power he was exerting over her. In a funny way it was comforting that there was this physical consequence, that he was taking this step to curtail her spending. She also felt somewhat reassured that he cared enough to do this.

A host of sensations were coming to the surface. There was a melding of moisture as her clit throbbed to the same rhythm as her pulse. She found her breathing becoming faster, more labored. Looking down she could see her nipples were erect, aching to be fondled and sucked.

She turned her gaze back to Alan, as he unfolded his arms and placed them casually in his pockets and again she thought she could see the merest flicker of a smile. She wondered if he was enjoying this.

She let her gaze drop, feeling reassured by the bulge in his trousers. She liked the thought of his building hunger. She was relieved to see that his desire for her was undiminished.

Emboldened by the thought of his lust, she reached to the side of her skirt and slid down the zip, giving an extra wiggle as she shimmied and the black fabric pooled at her feet. If she put on a good enough show maybe that would be enough. It warmed her to think he might just wrap her in his arms and forget about the spanking.

She bent, gave her ass a seductive wiggle before picking up the skirt and placing it on the chair. As she straightened she turned to Alan. She watched as a knowing smile spread over his face. She searched for a reason beyond him enjoying the extra wiggle of her ass. Then, with a stab of horror it dawned on her that he could see her wet panties. In the passion of the moment, her slight accident had slipped her mind. Her cheeks flushed hot with embarrassment and she felt a rush of humiliation at the thought that her weakness had been exposed.

He seemed to be enjoying her shame. She could not really see the fascination; he had seen her with and without panties many times before. His gaze seemed transfixed on her crotch and the damp stain. Maybe it was the naughtiness of her wetting herself that had him so captivated.

She wondered what turned him on more, her humiliation or the prospect of beating her. She felt the curious persistent throb, between her legs. There was a heaviness deep in her feminine core, a persistent nag that would not be silenced.

She could not remember the last time she had been this aroused. She wanted him.

There was silence and she hesitated for just a moment, and thought of asking Alan if he would relent. Maybe he would be pacified by her mouth or a nice soft fuck. She saw his brow start to furrow again and felt her hope dwindle. She had seen him mellow, if just a little. She wanted her lover back and she saw him in his smile and warm eyes. She definitely did not want to see him freeze over again.

Without a word she hooked her thumbs into the waistband of her panties and slid them down unhooking them from her feet before placing the thin white cotton with her other clothes.

She stood erect and naked. The dimple in his cheek betrayed his broadening smile and the crow's feet at the corners of Alan's eyes showed his admiration of her body. She basked in the glow of his approval. It had been such a long time since she'd felt it and she felt warmed by it now. It felt as if her husband was beginning to return to her.

"Very good." He paused and there was a joyous tone in his voice. It was as if he was revelling in this moment of her submission. The brief praise made her glow, warming her like a sip of hot chocolate on a winter's day. "I want you to go to the bedroom. I will join you in a few minutes."

Barbara nodded. "Yes Sir."

The wait in their bedroom was unbearable. She stood trembling as the silence was broken by the tap of his leather soles landing on the hardwood stairs. The sound got louder as the footsteps approached slowly, menacingly. She wanted to run, scream, cry, beg him to give her another chance but fear had rooted her to the spot.

The floorboard creaked as he left the wood and stepped onto the bedroom carpet. She smelled his musky aftershave even before she saw him enter the room. Barbara lifted her head to look at him. His shirt was bright in the comparative gloom and he stood in front of her with his arms folded across his broad chest. She felt powerless, like a leaf on a breeze and totally at his mercy.

He stood motionless looking at her but saying nothing. She felt manipulated but unable to do anything about it. She stifled a sob as a tear finally broke free from the corner of her eye.

She felt its wet path as it slid down her cheek.

The silence stretched on as she realized that him making her wait this way was also part of his power over her. She shivered nervously convinced that he must be enjoying this.

The well of emotions whirled inside her each fighting for her attention. It was true she was scared, but she also felt exhilarated about the idea of being called to account and punished and it troubled her. What kind of woman *wanted* to be spanked?

Alan's presence loomed large by the bed, his silence, added to the tension. She had never felt this helpless, so completely without power. Daddy had been cross with her, yet even when she was a child he had not disciplined her with corporal punishment. He had made rules, but he had never made a rule that she had not been able to bend to suit herself. Alan was different and she had never really mastered the art of winding him around her fingers.

He broke the silence, his words slow, the sound of controlled anger in his gravelly low voice.

"Barbara, we have talked before about your excessive spending and I thought I had made it plain that it was to stop. You have money to spend and I am not a tyrant. I want you to be happy." His words trailed off.

If he wanted to make her happy why the punishment? Why not simply stop bitching about the money? That would make her very happy.

There must have been something in her face that gave her thoughts away.

"I can see you are confused. Happiness is not about material things." He sighed. "I want to teach you that there is more to life than simply acquiring stuff. There is a joy in contentment, in restraint, in the simple things in life."

Alan's words made her feel bad about spending money, as if there was something foul and dirty about it. But there was an addictive quality to having that kind of power. It made her feel like she had with Alan at the beginning, so wanted, so needed. She loved the way the sales people followed her around. It made her feel special.

Why wouldn't Alan show her that kind of attention?

"I can see that you don't believe me." He inclined his head toward her, inviting her to speak.

She looked hard for the right words, but none came easily, "I don't know… There is something missing. I feel lonely. When I feel that way I shop. I can't explain it."

Alan looked serious. "I am trying to understand Barbara. I really do want you to be happy but I know that shopping is not the answer. Spending money on things we don't need is disrespectful." His expression was more hurt than angry.

It was something that until now she hadn't truly considered. She knew that her actions angered him, but she hadn't realized that they hurt him.

Alan came over to her and softly stroked her hair as he talked. "I feel

I have to lay down the law, and when I do you ignore me. What am I supposed to do with you? I have tried everything. Reasoning with you, arguing with you, even cutting up the credit card and yet nothing I say makes a scrap of difference. That is why I think a physical correction is necessary. I think it will get the message across."

Her heart sank, dread settling over her like a heavy dark fog that clogged her throat and squeezed her chest making it hard to get her thoughts into words. She was aware of the distance that had grown between them. She felt so sad that it had come to this. She wanted to be a good wife, but when they fought, or when Alan was away at sea the loneliness crept into her soul crowding out her good intentions.

She looked into her husband's eyes, as she stood there, stripped naked before him. It was not just that she was naked, she felt her soul exposed.

She looked up at him and saw the pained expression in his eyes. Her chest ached as she spoke. "I want to be happy too." She sighed, enjoying the soothing touch of his hand as he stroked her hair. "I want you to be happy, and I want you to be happy with me." Her voice cracked and she stifled a sob wondering if that were possible now. "I want it to be like it was in the beginning. I want you to be proud of me again."

The tension that had furrowed his brow had dissolved, his soft smile and warm eyes had returned. Alan wrapped his arms around her, covering her naked flesh with his body. It felt like coming home after a long trip away as she melted into his chest, felt his warm breath on her hair.

"I am so proud of you." He whispered the words, his mind catching on the things that made him proudest. He loved her dedication to organizations that helped the poor and the sick. He admired her tenacity. He'd never seen her let financial obstacles stand in the way when it came to one of her charities. He'd seen her cajole and chide her way through her parent's circle of acquaintances getting them to give time and money to support one of her charities. He stroked her cheek. He was proud of her. Damned proud.

"I love you. I always have and I always will, but that doesn't mean that I am happy about $1500 shoes."

He truly felt that this was a turning point, though he debated whether he should spank her, wondering if it would sour the reconciliation that had happened between them.

Even so he wanted to cement their newfound commitment in a very physical way. He didn't want to hurt her but he knew from deep down inside that a physical punishment would make their union even stronger. A line needed to be drawn.

He took in a deep breath and let it out slowly. His big hands took her shoulders, holding her so their eyes met. "I do love you and I do want to make everything right between us. But that said, retail therapy is not the answer." He ran his fingers through her hair, then stroked down her cheek. He enjoyed the feel of her soft skin as he took hold of her chin and lifted her gaze to meet his. "There is a lesson to be learned and the shoes have to be paid for, one way or another." His voice trailed off. There was a hint of resolute determination in it. "I am wanting to draw a line under this incident so that we can move on."

Barbara gave him a half smile. Although she was complying he could sense her uneasiness with the idea.

"I think this needs to be done. Are you willing to submit?"

She heard no malice in his voice, just the tone of a task that had to be done.

"Yes Sir," her voice sounded shaky even to her own ears.

"Freely? And willingly?"

The tremble that worked through her made her voice wobble. "Yes Sir."

She didn't *want* him to spank her, but she felt there was no alternative. She wanted to get her life back to normal, put the past behind and start over and if this was the way she would do whatever it took to set things right. "I will do whatever you ask, of my own free will."

"Good girl, I am pleased that you will submit." She felt the warmth of his hand, as he stroked her cheek softly, reassuring her of the need for this action. "I know you are reluctant; this is your first time. I know you are scared because you don't know what is going to happen, but I hope you will come to see that this is for your own good."

Although his words sounded sincere, she could not reconcile in her own mind, the two sides of the coin, his words of love and his need to inflict punishment. But then again she could not tie together why the thought of this scared her and aroused her at the same time. Maybe it was the same for him.

She looked up for a moment and saw him standing there, menacing, totally in control. In his hands she saw he was holding a length of pink rope and the riding crop.

Alan straightened himself to his full height, feeling the muscles in his back flex, "So my pet, with this punishment we have a new start. The slate wiped clean."

He looked down at Barbara. Her head was lowered in natural submission, yet there was a part of her that still seemed strong and defiant. Despite the disobedience there was something about her strength he admired. He also felt that in some way he had played his part in this situation. If he had not been so indulgent in their early days together, if he had been clear about what he wanted in the first place, shown her more attention, then maybe it would not have gone this far.

"Look up please." His gaze caught hers. He saw the worry in her chocolaty brown eyes and felt a wave of concern that this was too much.

"I know this is hard for you, but it is for the best." He saw her tremble as she watched him place the crop on the bed. Her lip quivered as he picked up the pink silk rope and stretched a section of the cord between his clenched fists.

He gestured to the bedroom dressing stool in the middle of the bedroom. "I want you to lay over the stool please."

She gave him an apprehensive sideways glance.

He took a step back to give her room to position herself. He allowed himself a smile as he watched with satisfaction and a sense of pride as she complied with his instruction.

He watched as her soft breasts pushed against the velvety covering on the small backless stool, trying to imagine how the soft material felt against her smooth skin. His dexterous fingers tied her to the stool with the pink silk rope. He hoped in time the restraints would not be necessary, but for the first time he did not want her wriggling about. His eyes wandered over her, apprehensively. She looked so submissive and he found her vulnerability arousing, yet he was aware of the responsibility that weighed on his shoulders.

Holding the riding crop at either end he flexed the shaft in his hands. It was pleasingly subtle. He remembered the excitement of finding the crop and the thrill the first time he swiped the air with it. He loved the swish, loved the way the tightly bound thin strips of leather felt in his hand. Feeling it now he recalled practicing with it first on a pillow and then on his hand. Over time he had progressed to his own thigh. The thought of the sting still made his thigh ache.

Alan viciously swiped at the air with the crop, loving both the sound it made and the way it made her twitch and flinch in anticipation of a swipe landing on her. "Now my pet, it is time to answer for your misdemeanors."

He liked the fact she was expecting the worst, but he felt he could not use the crop, not this first time anyway. He considered it a step too far too soon.

He shook the tension out of his shoulders and took up a pose, readying himself before he struck. The first strike was with the flat of his hand on her right ass cheek. He was surprised at the sting in his own hand but he liked the satisfying sound of flesh on flesh and the heat that radiated through his own palm.

She let out a little yelp, he guessed more out of surprise than any pain or discomfort. He hadn't struck that hard. He wanted to start slowly, testing how she would react to his hand striking her bottom.

He enjoyed the idea of surprising her, never really letting her know what was going to happen next. He landed a second spank on her other cheek. He liked the feeling of her hot skin on his hot hand.

His second spank landing was accompanied by her letting out a gasp and then a low whimper.

He lifted his palm and took the time to observe with pride the two hand prints on her peachy skin. His penis twitched in the tight confines of his pants. A third spank landed with a juicy slap, reddening her skin further and making Barbara suck in a breath. With the fourth spank, her skin began to glow a pleasing pink.

He found that as the color deepened, his penis got harder. After all the time of feeling impotent, unable to tame her he finally felt in control. .

"Please Sir!" Her voice was ragged. "Pleeeeeease, no more"

He ignored her plea and with each spank he felt more spiritually uplifted more in charge of the situation.

His hand landed again, she wriggled against her bonds "Please, Sir... Please stop... Please..."

The spanking was surely not hard enough to injure her, though he expected it stung. He did not want to hurt her, but he did want to drive home the point, remind her who was in charge. He kept a mental note of the number of strikes. Seven and her bottom was a cherry pink. He felt her tremble beneath him, she wriggled and resisted. It was a wonderful feeling to exercise this level of control and restraint.

"Sir! It hurts Sir! I promise to be good."

Alan again, assessed the intensity of his swats and considered them strong enough to sting, but not to injure her, yet she continued to plead for mercy. He determined that if the spanking was to do any good, it should be a lesson that would be remembered.

As Alan landed the ninth, he paid special attention to not striking on any of the previous marks, his goal was to get an even shade, from the tops of her thighs to the top of her buttocks.

"Sir, please, I won't do it again."

More spanks fell and although she still pleaded and struggled, it seemed to him that her struggles had lost some of their intensity.

Alan's heart pounded in his chest, his breath felt tight in his throat. He noticed a bead of sweat trickle down his brow. Until then he had not considered how much physical effort he was expending. He enjoyed the buzzy feeling it gave him, that endorphin rush urged him on. The next spank was a tad harder.

Barbara let out a little squeal, it didn't sound like pain, more like she was enjoying it, or at least was resigned to it.

Urged on, he felt a sweet ache in his groin. His hand adjusted his penis in an attempt to make himself more comfortable. He could see that he was not the only one to be receiving pleasure from the spanking. He noticed a dribble of sweet nectar moistening her nether lips. The small mewing noises she made seemed now to be more the moans of pleasure. It pleased him to think this was not one sided. He stopped spanking and noticed his hand ached. He imagined it must be the same for her ass. He slowly ran a finger along her labia. She moaned and he felt her push back. She really was enjoying this. He slipped his moist finger inside and softly stroked in and out.

"How are you doing?"

Her voice was hesitant. "I am fine Sir." Her hips pushing back and forth showed how very turned on she was. She certainly didn't seem to be any worse for this experience, in fact quite the contrary she actually seemed to be enjoying it. He looked at her reddening bottom. He considered stopping there and taking her from behind, picturing himself buried inside her, his stomach pushed tight to her warm bottom. The idea was very potent, the position very dominant, he'd be truly in the driving seat. He wanted her but decided to wait, resisting the urge for instant gratification.

"How do you feel?" he asked, hoping the warmth of his feelings came out in his voice.

"I feel fine Sir." Her voice sounded more confident now.

"I think you like it…the spanking, not my finger." She said nothing but wiggled her hips and gave him a little smile as she looked over her shoulder. "Do you want more?" He paused. "Pain then pleasure?"

"Yes Sir," she answered, her voice low and seductive.

"Pain then pleasure?"

"Yes Sir," she repeated, her voice husky with need.

The sound of her voice filled with desire, fueled his own need. He wanted her more now than any time he could remember. It took all his willpower not to make love to her then and there. As he withdrew his finger, she let out a little whine, obviously missing the digit. He wiped the wetness on the warmed reddened skin of her ass. He landed another affectionate spank sweetly on her left cheek.

She missed the feel of his hand when it stopped spanking. She craved Alan's attention. She shuddered when she felt his fingers touch her sensitive, swollen labia, hungered for him to take her, to possess her.

"How does my little girl like this?" His voice was warm with affection.

She couldn't manage more than a mew of contentment. Loving the feeling of his strong dominant fingers as he slowly fondled her clit. The sensation was driving her wild, it was like pins and needles playing on her skin, yet at the same time being stroked with a piece of silk. His finger was at the entrance of her treasure and she could not resist the urge to push back, wantonly impaling herself onto his erect digit.

"Yes, my girl, is hungry, isn't she?" His tone encouraged her.

"Hmmmm, yes Sir… God yes…" She was sopping wet, and the throb in her clit was driving her crazy. She desperately wanted to cum and she knew he was deliberately denying her orgasm.

"Does my little girl want more?" There was a tease in his voice.

"Mmm… Please Sir… I'll do anything Sir… Please Sir…" She would joyfully agree to anything, just so long as he wouldn't stop. She felt the fire growing inside her and felt herself close to the edge. Just a little further and she would surrender to her building orgasm.

Suddenly the sensations stopped and the finger was removed, her pleasure denied.

"Sir?" There was desperation in her voice.

"Silence… Not a word." His words were commanding.

She stayed quiet, but God! What was he doing? He'd stopped! She wanted to plead, beg, but there was no doubt that he was in command. She felt his finger, slick with her wetness, wipe over her bottom. The moisture cooled her ass cheek.

She lay there alone with her thoughts, physically empty, hungry and wanting, waiting, at his mercy, consumed with a mix of excitement and apprehension.

The first thing Barbara knew of the change from his hand to the crop, was the bee sting on her ass. She felt the electricity buzz through her and the fire was stoked again.

Another sting bit. She loved the way he made her feel. It was curiously liberating handing the control to Alan.

Barbara let out a little gasp as the third swat of the crop landed and her buttocks clenched, sending little electric shock waves through her body. She should hate this, yet she didn't. She felt surprisingly comforted by the restraints, it was like being healed, forgiven. What was it Alan had said, the slate wiped clean?

She was calmed by the mixture of feelings, pleasure and pain in equal measure. She loved the tingly feeling in her bottom and the insistent throb of her clit as the crop bit. The initial discomfort and humiliation had given way to a warm throb deep in her center. The warmth had grown to a fire that spread though her body.

It seemed inappropriate to actually enjoy corporal punishment. Yet there it was, she found it curiously pleasurable to submit to this. She welcomed the sweet and sour, the sugar dissolving in the vinegar, the subtle mixture of pain and pleasure.

Another bee stung her tender ass. She felt intoxicated. Thoughts wandered into her mind in the hazy way they do after couple of glasses of wine. Had she bought the shoes to deliberately provoke him?

Of course she had never had this in mind. She had never seen Alan in quite this way before, but she had been aware of his power, his intransigence and how much his assertiveness turned her on.

Another sting of the crop and she felt the sparks of desire fly. Her pubis found the edge of the stool. Instinctively she ground her mound on it; she felt the hard edge contrasting with the soft fabric. This newly added stimulation was just enough to get her right on the edge, but not quite enough to make her tumble into the abyss of the orgasm she so desperately needed. She tried to push harder but the promised land she craved eluded her.

A cool breeze caught the trickle of liquid on her inner thigh. Her breath caught in her throat as the bite of another crop strike caught her between her cheeks. Her body was alive as the electric sparks flew once more.

Rolling waves of pleasure set up a slow penetrating rhythm deep in her centre, contrasting with the sharp spikes the crop burnt into her flesh. The rhythm pushed her closer and closer to the cliff edge. She felt the pins and needles in her skin, the rough and smooth the threshold of climax. She surrendered herself totally to him as she toppled over the invisible edge into the pit of carnal lust.

She swooned, as the first vinegary tingles washed over her. The bitter sweet waves tingled, from the tips of her fingers to the tips of her toes. She was lost in a sensory overload that cascaded over her. Muscles clenched and relaxed in throbbing cascades of sensation. She felt the hardness of her teeth clench on the softness of her lower lip. A wash of colors sounds and textures filled her mind. Soft, hard, sweet, bitter. The world became a timeless place. An explosion that burned white hot and cool all at the same time. She felt as if she was melting away. Bliss enveloped her in warm waves.

Alan felt himself breathing heavily. There was an ache in his arm and the exertion had soaked his shirt with perspiration. For now at least he regarded the tigress within her had been tamed. He felt contented and centered. He wanted to hold the lady he loved. Then he wanted to make long slow love to her, to make her his again. He wanted her to see him as the giver of pleasure, as well as pain. He wanted to be everything to her. Protector and Master.

He looked at her flaccid over the stool and worried that he had gone too far this first time. Had he been too rough? Had he hurt her? His mind bubbled with questions as he untied her. Through his concern he looked at her punished bottom and took a certain pride in the accuracy of the pattern of welts on her ass. The design was beginning to spread and merge, as the bruises came out, joining together in a kaleidoscope of colors.

He spread out his favorite bathroom towel on the bed to protect the Egyptian cotton sheets, lifted her onto the towel and softly massaged oil into her bottom. She lay passively, as he enjoyed the feel of her peachy skin reddened and heated by his chastisement. He felt immensely proud that she had bourn the punishment without verbal complaint. His fingers made patterns in the oil that soothed his hand which had been reddened by the spanking.

With her surrender to him, he felt that this would be a new beginning for them, or at least he hoped so. Maybe the spankings would be a feature of their love making. For the moment he was content to be with her, so close, so together.

The world slowly returned to Barbara. Her mind was fuzzy. Like waking from a dream, realities began to dawn on her. She was no longer on the floor, tied. Alan must have untied her and carried her to the bed without her realizing it. She was laying face down on a fluffy towel and he was affectionately massaging a soothing and sweet smelling balm into her tender, punished flesh.

She knew, as she had right at the start, that she loved Alan with all her heart. He was her rock, the man that provided all the love and structure she could possibly need. The chastisement really would be a turning point…good for her… good for them. He had been right all along.

Nadia Nautalia

Meredith's First Spanking

Brant leaned against the worn vinyl back of his chair in the diner as he listened to the other ranchers discussing ranch business. When the topics of weather, cattle, and the price of winter feed had been exhausted, the conversation drifted toward the topic of the wives of the other men gathered around the table.

In the past Brant had ignored this part of the conversation. Always before he'd felt that he had nothing of value to add. As a newlywed, he was one of the few members of the group that hadn't embraced spanking as a way to keep his wife in line. As a result he'd endured a fair amount of good-natured ribbing about being smitten and spoiling his new bride.

Today he listened more intently to the conversations about the other men's wives and how they'd been called to task. In the past day and a half, he'd begun to think maybe the older men who'd been married longer did know something he didn't. It was sure as shit that he needed to do something about Meredith. As he listened to Sam talk about caning and grounding his wife for her latest speeding ticket, his frustration with Meredith gnawed at him, making him feel short-tempered and irritable.

Two days before he'd opened a letter from Meredith's cosmetology school which had contained her grades. The envelope *had* been addressed to her, and by rights he supposed he shouldn't have opened it. He wouldn't have had it not looked like the quarterly tuition bill and had he not been sitting down to pay some ranch bills.

Even though he knew he shouldn't have opened the letter, he couldn't forget the fact that Meredith's grades were all D's and that she'd missed about one quarter of her classes. What bothered him even more than the poor grades and poor attendance was the fact that she'd been lying to him for weeks. Every time he'd asked her about school she'd replied that it was going "fine" and changed the subject.

Now that he knew that she'd been lying he wanted to confront her at the very least. The more he listened to the other men guffaw about their own exploits with their wives and the manner in which they'd corrected their behavior, the more his hand itched to light a fire on her ass.

"I thrashed Brooke a good one last weekend," Jake Humbolt said around a bite of cherry pie."She invited her whole family up for the weekend and didn't tell me about it till the night before they were due to arrive."

"Wives," Butch sighed. "Mine has had some kind of a burr under her saddle. I don't know what's going on with her, but she's been about as cranky as a horse with a burr under its saddle." He frowned. "I guess I'm going to have to break down and paddle her ass if she doesn't get out of this pissy-assed mood."

"Well I don't think mine'll be inviting the family up again without asking anytime soon." Jake grinned. "Blistered her ass and made her wear a remote controlled butt plug the whole time her family was there."

"You're evil," Sam guffawed.

"So I've been told." Jake grinned.

"What about you Brant? Meredith still towing the line?"

Brant drew a deep breath, feeling torn about how much to share with his friends, but truth be told he wanted their advice. "Well… not so much," he drawled. "Found out this morning that she's been missing a bunch of her classes and is close to failing. I'm sure as hell tempted to warm her backside."

Several of the men around the table nodded. "Yeah, you gotta nip that kinda thing in the bud, hard and fast," Jake said. "Nothing quite does it like a good hard spanking. But I find it takes a little more than just the spanking."

"Like the plug?" Brant asked imagining Meredith's protests if he suggested putting a plug in her ass.

Jake nodded. "Yes, or grounding her like Sam did with his wife, or sending her to bed early every night, or making her write lines, or keep a journal of her school work. There are lots of things you can do besides just spanking her that will remind her after the spanking that you're the one in charge."

"Thing is, wives need to know that they can count on us to bring them back in line when they get out of line. You have to be a bit of a hard ass about it. They'll whine and cry and beg and promise to be good, but if you stop spanking before she's learned her lesson...you'll be right back spanking her again in a day or two. Not that that's a hardship mind you." Sam grinned.

"It's the other things, grounding, being sent to bed early or maintenance spankings that remind her who is boss over the long haul though."

Brant nodded, his mind going to the whippings he'd received from his father when he'd been a boy. The razor strap his father had used had hurt like a son of a bitch, but it had kept him on the straight and narrow. He wondered if Meredith needed the same kind of control and guidance from him that he'd needed from his father.

* * * *

When he came in from the ranch chores that evening, Meredith was already in the kitchen with dinner almost ready. She wore a white tank top and cut-off shorts that emphasized the roundness of her butt, the length of her legs, and the healthy tan of her skin. Just looking at her was enough to make Brant's heart catch. He still felt like the luckiest man on the planet to have such a beautiful, sexy woman for a wife.

He poured the drinks and put the salad dressing and steak sauce on the table, and then sat down to wait for Meredith to finish serving the rest of the meal. As she cooked she chatted about plans for the Labor Day barbecue they were hosting. He enjoyed her enthusiasm as he was looking forward to it too. There'd be music and dancing, and it'd be a chance to relax with friends. Even so there was a pall cast over the event by the knowledge that she'd been lying to him, repeatedly, for weeks. The knowledge was an irritant that he couldn't quite dislodge.

He'd had all day to stew over the advice the other ranchers had given him. He'd decided he needed to confront Meredith about her lies, her grades, and her attendance. He figured he could make a decision about what to do about it all based on her reaction.

His stomach was a ball of nerves, both because he hated confrontation and because he wasn't sure how Meredith would react to the news that he was going to spank her, if it came to that. He really didn't want to fight with his bride. Yet, he knew that if his father had been swayed by the fact that he didn't want to be strapped with the razor strap when he was a youngster, he might have started skipping school and drinking beer like some of his friends had. He knew without a doubt his life would have turned out different if he'd taken that alternative route.

He owed it to Meredith to do what was best for her, and what was best for their marriage. He simply couldn't tolerate her lying to him. A marriage couldn't survive constant dishonestly. He would confront her, get to the bottom of it, and dole out whatever discipline was necessary. Then they'd put it behind them.

Meredith put the plates of food on the table and slid into her spot, eager to steer the conversation toward Brant's day and away from hers. She hoped he wouldn't ask about her day. She'd arrived at school late again, so she'd gone shopping instead. There had been a few things to pick up for the Labor Day barbecue so the time hadn't been totally wasted. Still, she'd felt guilty every time he'd asked her about school for weeks. The stock answer that it was going "fine" was really no longer true. Her grades were bad. She'd be kicked out soon if she didn't catch up the work she was behind on.

"This looks delicious," Brant said, picking up his knife and fork and cutting into his steak.

"Thanks." She smiled. "How was your day?"

Brant seemed to take a long time answering. The way he chewed, methodically, as if thinking about how to answer made her stomach feel funny, the way it felt at the top of a roller coaster, just before it plunged down.

"Fine, how was yours?" he asked after a minute of silent chewing.

She shrugged. "Okay I guess."

"School?"

She sighed. "It was there, but I don't really want to talk about school."

"You don't want to talk about it? Hmm…" He put another chunk of meat in his mouth, chewed and swallowed.

Somehow the slow way he responded made her feel like a bug trapped under a magnifying glass, as if he already knew she'd cut class that day…or worse.

"Could that have to do with the fact you've missed about a quarter of your classes and your grades are in the basement?"

His tone was low; the irritation in his voice grated along her nerves. She bristled, feeling ashamed of her school performance and defensive at the same time. "What business is it of yours?" she blustered. "I'm not a little girl, and you're not my daddy. It's not up to you to make sure I go to school like a good little girl."

"What business is it of mine?" He put down his fork and fixed her with an intense stare that pinned her in place. "What business is it of mine?"

Her mind spun. How had he found out about her grades and her attendance? Clearly he was not happy with, her but how much did he know, and how was she going to do damage control without knowing what he knew?

"Well, let's see, little girl. Besides the fact that you're my wife, and you've lied to me for weeks, I'm the one that pays the tuition." He snapped his fingers as if he'd forgotten something. "And oh yeah, I'm the one that pays for the car that you drive to school…when you can be bothered to go. "

She hated it when he called her little girl. It reminded her of the teenage crush she'd had on him and the way she'd followed him around like a lost puppy.

"I'm not your little girl. I'm your wife. Your equal," she snapped.

He raised an eyebrow? "Really? My equal? Where's your contribution to the household?" He picked up his knife and cut into his steak again. "You agreed it was important for you to have something to fall back on. You wanted to go to cosmetology school. I agreed to that. Come to find out you've missed a quarter of your classes and lied about it to boot."

His disappointment washed over her, making her feel like a gawky teenager unworthy of his attention. She sighed. "I'm sorry."

"I'm sure you are, Meredith." She heard his sigh and felt the intensity of his gaze as he stared at her with an intense, unwavering stare. "But this discussion isn't over, not by a long shot. Finish your dinner. When you're done come find me in the bedroom. We'll finish our discussion there."

Her stomach did a tight little summersault. The firmness and finality in his voice left no room for argument. His attitude reminded her of the way her father had sounded when she'd misbehaved. Her father's bouts of firmness had usually preceded a spanking.

Her heart sped up. Her palms grew sweaty. She drew them along the legs of her cut-offs. Surely Brant didn't intend to spank her. He was her husband, not her daddy. But if he didn't intend to spank her, why did he want her to find him in the bedroom? She was sure he was in no frame of mind to want sex.

The idea of his big, powerful, calloused hands guiding her over his lap and holding her in place as he reigned spanks over her bottom flirted around the edges of her mind. The idea made her stomach dance in a combination of dread and something else she couldn't quite identify.

"Please Brant, I'm sorry. It won't happen again. I know I was wrong to lie about school all this time," she said as he stood up and carried his plate to the sink.

Brant's anger at her selfishness began to dissolve at the pleading tone in her voice. He was sure she *was* sorry now that she'd been caught. However, if he'd not caught her he doubted she'd be confessing. She had continued to lie right up to the point he'd let her know he knew about her grades and attendance.

Even so, the intense desire to grab her and blister her ass till she couldn't sit for a week had ebbed. In its place was the knowledge that this was something he needed to do, for her, for their relationship. He *needed* to do to take charge of her, of the situation. He needed to show leadership, to get her back on track, and to create closure for both of them. She needed to pay for messing up at school and lying about it so that she could start again with a clean slate.

"I love you Meredith, and I'll expect to see you upstairs when you've finished dinner."

* * * *

Meredith had dragged her feet for as long as she could. She'd no longer felt like eating after Brant left the table, but she'd taken her time cleaning the kitchen and putting the dishes away. She'd felt unsettled, and uncertain, as skittish as an unbroken foal as she'd contemplated the balance of their discussion.

She reached the top of the steps and peeked into the bedroom where Brant sat on the side of the bed waiting for her. "Come here," he said, patting the bed beside him.

She moved slowly into the room, feeling like a fly flirting with the edge of a spider web as she crossed to the bed and plopped down beside him.

He turned toward her and, lifting a hand, he pushed the hair back away from her face and tipped her chin so that she had no choice but to meet his gaze. "We've already established that you missed a bunch of your classes, haven't done your homework, and are close to failing your classes, and that you've been lying to me about it. You've told me that you are sorry and I believe that you are. But sometimes in a relationship when one party does harm to the relationship there needs to be a rebalancing of sorts."

"What do you want me to do? I've already said I'm sorry." Frustration churned within her. She'd owned up, she'd apologized, what more did he want?

He took her hand and squeezed it gently. "I'm going to spank you, Meredith, long and hard."

Her stomach dropped. There was fear, dread, and uncertainty but also a tightness deep in her core that wasn't unlike the arousal she felt when he touched her in bed.

"Please Brant. Give me another chance. I'll get caught up at school," she begged, knowing she didn't really deserve another chance but feeling compelled to beg anyway.

"Sorry, little girl. I want you to think about the damage that you did to our relationship by not holding up your end of your school commitments and by lying."

The breath hitched in her chest as the knowledge that he really intended to spank her sunk in.

"Now stand up," he ordered.

She stood in front of him feeling like a naughty little girl. "Shorts off," he said, making short work of the button and the zipper. "Panties, too," he added, as she slipped the cutoffs down her legs.

Her heart seemed to be pounding in her ears. Her fingers felt numb as she pushed at the elastic band of her panties.

"Here you go," he said, tugging the panties the rest of the way down her legs and pulling her into place across his lap.

She quivered as he slid his hand over her bottom and sucked in a sharp breath as his hand raised. She let her breath out on a squeal as his hand connected sharply with her bottom leaving a sting in its wake. "It's bad enough you didn't get to school and that your grades are what they are." He spanked twice more in quick succession to punctuate his words.

The spanks stung, but she knew they were no more than she deserved, so she accepted them without complaint.

Four more spanks fell quickly in their wake, intensifying the burn. "What's worse is that you lied to me, not once, but again and again."

He spanked her again, but this time there was a crack and the burn was more intense and spread out more. She looked back over her shoulder and saw that he held a wooden paddle. He spanked steadily, covering every part of her bottom and upper thighs till she felt like her whole bottom was on fire.

Suddenly, there was nothing erotic about the spanking. It hurt, pure and simple. She wriggled in his grasp and he continued to spank her. The pain continued to build, and she began to worry that he'd just continue spanking her till she couldn't take it anymore. She wondered what would happen when she reached the point she couldn't take any more. Would she cry? Beg? Pass out?

Her dad had certainly never spanked her like this. His spankings had been short and mild by comparison. "Please. Ouch. I'm sorry," she begged.

"I am sure you are sorry. But this isn't about being sorry. This is about making up for the wrong you did…it's about paying for the damage you did to our relationship, to my trust."

His words wormed their way into her, leaving a heavy sadness and shame in their wake. She'd hurt their relationship, lied to him, all because she'd been too disorganized to get to school on time.

He spanked five or six more times in steady cadence, spreading and intensifying the sting that made her twist and turn on his lap as she tried to avoid the searing pain that erupted where he spanked. "Do you think I'll trust you next time you tell me something?"

"No. Probably not," she cried. The knowledge that she'd really damaged their marriage made her feel small and hopeless.

"No, that's right. You hurt our marriage. You damaged my trust in you." He spanked her again and again, so many times she lost track of how many times the wicked paddle connected with her stinging bottom before it dropped lower to spread the searing sting across her upper thighs.

The panic within her grew as the sting and the burn grew more intense. She was sure she had to have welts all over her bottom from the paddle. "Please," she begged. "What do you want me to do? I'll do it. Just stop." Tears that had already been running down her face turned to full blown sobs. "Please, Brant." She wriggled and kicked her feet to no avail. He just tightened his grip and spanked harder.

"That's just it. There is nothing you can *do*. All you can do is accept this spanking and learn from it."

Her mind stumbled and struggled. What did he mean? What did

he want her to do? What would make it stop? Did he mean he wouldn't stop? Surely he had to stop sometime. But if he went on much longer, she wouldn't be able to walk when he did stop.

The tears cascaded down her face, and the sobs deepened as the pain and the knowledge that she couldn't stop it grew.

He'd said accept the spanking. Learn from it. She was accepting it... but how was she supposed to learn from it?

As he struck her harder, letting the pain radiate outward, making her anticipate the next spank, she realized she wasn't really accepting the punishment. She was focused on trying to twist, squirm, and escape the sizzling swats that landed over her bottom and thighs spreading the burn all the way to her knees.

Accept the spanking. Learn from it. The words he'd said morphed into a chant in her mind. She struggled to relax into the pain, accepting it as her due rather than fighting against it. She steeled herself to welcome the pain rather than fighting to avoid the stinging swats.

As she relaxed into the knowledge that she could do nothing to avoid the pain being inflicted on her, and that she deserved it, her sobs softened. She realized there was a certain peace in accepting the spanking rather than fighting against it. Her sobs were no longer intended to make him stop. Instead they were cleansing sobs...sobs that expressed the physical pain she felt and the deep sorrow she felt over the damage she had done her marriage with her lies.

She would never be certain when he stopped spanking her and began to rub her blazing bottom. She became aware of it sometime after the spanking had stopped, while she'd cried brokenly into the mattress.

"I'm so sorry I lied. I won't ever do it again," she cried as she welcomed his gentle touch even though even the light touches on her bottom and legs burned like fire.

"I know, little one. I know." His voice was soft, husky, as if he too fought against tears. "You're forgiven."

She continued to cry softly as his hands slid gently over her bottom and back. She wanted and needed his tenderness, and the soft words of forgiveness he uttered.

"I want you to kneel on the bed on your hands and knees facing the headboard for me," he said when her sobs had died down.

"Why?" she sniffed.

"Because I'm going to insert a plug to remind you that you're my wife, that I love you, and that you can tell me the truth about anything and I won't love you any less."

Her heart began to pound. Her mind raced. "A-a- plug? What kind of plug?"

"A plug." He stroked her from her shoulders to her bottom. "It goes in your bottom…to serve as a reminder…"

"I don't know if…"

"I don't remember asking, Meredith. It's part of your punishment. I really don't want to have to spank you again, but I will if you choose to argue with me."

"I don't know why you want…"

"Because I decided that it's what you needed as part of your punishment." He sighed. "Get into position. Now!"

His tone of voice booked no argument, and she had no desire to feel the wrath of the paddle again, so she eased herself off his lap, stifling a moan as the punished skin of her ass protested movement.

With no other option but to obey him, she climbed onto the bed and positioned herself on her hands and knees facing the headboard as he'd requested. Her stomach felt knotted and tight with a mixture of arousal, dread, and embarrassment.

"Is it going to hurt?" she asked, as he moved behind her.

"Probably some, but I'll be as gentle as I can." His hand on her back pressed her down onto the bed till her breasts rested against the bed and her bottom stuck up. Then he urged her farther knees apart.

The position wasn't uncomfortable, but it was embarrassing. She felt as if she were on display, open and vulnerable in a way she had never been before.

"Take deep breaths and relax. I'm going to lube you up back here so the plug will slide in."

She really didn't want this, but she swallowed hard and nodded. The feeling of being at the top of the hill on the roller coaster prepared for the sudden plunge to the bottom was back. She bit her lip as she felt his fingers on her bottom gently spreading her cheeks apart. Though his touch was generally gentle, it still stung where he touched her. She closed her eyes, stifling a moan as she felt his finger at her back entrance slowly exerting pressure.

It didn't really hurt as such. But there was a definite pressure and a feeling of discomfort that urged her to fight him, to block his entry into her most private place.

"Relax, honey. If you tighten up and fight me, it will only hurt more."

She tried to relax, she really did, but she found it impossible as his finger pressed into her rectum, slowly moving in and out, around and around. There was pressure and a small amount of pain as his finger moved in and out spreading the lube. "That's my good girl," he crooned softly. She relaxed then, wanting to please him, wanting to deserve his praise once again.

He withdrew his finger, relubed it and inserted it again. It was less painful this time, and she was able to relax, even enjoying the thrust of his finger as it moved in and out, teasing its way past the tight ring of muscle and back out again.

"Good girl," he said softly, withdrawing his finger once again.

She relaxed, repositioning her knees almost but not quite welcoming his finger once again. "Here comes the plug, baby," he said softly. She felt the tip hard against her rear opening and fought the urge to tighten up. The plug unlike his finger was hard and didn't give. It also seemed bigger, the pressure more intense as he pushed it into her opening.

Her body didn't accept it as readily and fought back with a sharp pain as he tried to push past the tight ring of muscle that guarded her back entrance.

He pressed the plug firmly against her opening, rocking it gently in and out as her tissues slowly opened, admitting more and more of the awful plug. As he rocked it in and out, the pain grew and intensified with each thrust inward. She bit her lip and fought the pain.

"Ouch…it hurts," she whimpered. "Ouch. Please."

"I know it hurts, and I'm sorry it does, but it is almost there." He continued to rock the horrible thing in and out, in and out in spite of her pleas and tears. "It is going in. You are going to take it."

"It hurts," she cried.

"You're so close. Relax a little more for me," he coached.

The pain spiraled and grew as he pushed the plug deeper and deeper, stretching her tissues. "I can't relax. It hurts too much."

"You can and you will."

She closed her eyes and tears began to squeeze through her lashes onto the bed. She was aware of Brant's hand on her back gently stroking her, soothing, comforting, even as he made her take the plug deeper into her body.

"That's my good girl. I'm so proud of you," he whispered, as he simultaneously rubbed her back and pushed the plug a little deeper. "You're almost there. Another good push and it'll be there."

Soft moans issued from her as he rubbed her back, her bottom, and then pushed the plug a little deeper.

She could feel her body beginning to loosen, to admit the plug and suddenly, she wanted it to be inside, fully seated. She wanted to please Brant, to hear his throaty praise once again.

When he pressed it in the next time, she pushed backward, pressing through the sharp pain to the miraculous feeling of her body fully yielding and the plug sliding home.

"Good girl! You did it, babe," he whispered near her ear. "How does it feel now?"

"Full…very full. It hurts a little bit, but nothing like it did going in." She turned her head and looked up at him aware of the tears that still danced on her eyelashes.At any other time she would have been embarrassed to have him see her tears, but now they felt like a badge of honor…a gift she had given him. She'd accepted the pain he'd given her, both the spanking and the plug and she was better for it.

"Good." He smiled. "I'm very proud of you for taking that so well."

Her heart swelled with pleasure. She felt clean and whole, as if the damage caused by her lies had been washed away by the spanking, by the tears, and by the experience of having to accept everything he'd dealt out simply because he had decided that she would accept it.

She felt her chest expand with love and newfound respect for her husband as she thought back over the way he had taken her in hand. She'd not started out wanting the spanking, and while he'd been spanking her she'd wanted nothing more than for it to stop, but there was something about the experience that transcended the physical. Being spanked and plugged made her feel safe and secure in the knowledge that her husband could and would handle whatever misbehavior she threw at him. She realized she liked that feeling.

Nadia Nautalia

A New Way Forward

"Abby, come in here please," Bryce hollered from the bedroom.

Abby heaved a sigh. She was right in the middle of answering an email from a potential client asking about her credentials and she wasn't thrilled about being interrupted. "Just a minute," she called back, continuing to type in short, frustrated bursts.

"Now." Bryce yelled from the bedroom, his voice brooking no argument and offering no patience.

Heaving another sigh Abby stood and walked to the bedroom. "What?" she asked irritably as she pushed the bedroom door open. Her breath caught in her throat. Bryce sat on the edge of the bed a cane and several papers in his hand.

Abby knew she should feel afraid, nervous, but it had been a long time since Bryce had spanked her and what she really felt was a tight, fluttery sensation deep in her center.

"Strip, and kneel on the bed. Now." Bryce said standing up. He moved around the room, pausing to stare pointedly at the four baskets of folded laundry that sat on the floor, then moving to the dresser where he ran his finger across the top of the dresser. "It's a bit dusty love," he said. "My slave hasn't been doing her job has she?"

"Um, I guess not Sir. I've been busy," she said, easing smoothly into the familiar game. She slipped her bra off and slid her panties over her hips, her heart pounding in anticipation.

She moved toward the bed, climbing onto the thick mattress, sinking to her knees on the bed as she watched her husband of seven years. Her heart pounded in her chest and she felt wetness seep from her pussy to coat her thighs as she waited, wishing that he was this forceful, this serious with her all the time.

"Down. With your breasts on the bed. Ass up, legs spread. Eyes down. Palms up." Her head spun. He'd never been this specific about her position before. His control over her placement made her feel mastered, controlled, and ultimately submissive. She was happy to have him demand more than the sloppy submission she usually presented him. She bent at the waist, pressing her breasts against the bed as he'd demanded, and scooting her legs apart as he'd requested. What was it he'd said about her eyes and palms?

"Eyes down. I don't want to see them unless I tell you to look at me," he said. She dipped her head feeling the power of his control wrapping around her tightening, compressing, like an elastic bandage stretched tightly around her chest.

"Arms out. Palms up," he instructed.

"Yes Sir," she whispered, knowing he liked to hear her call him that.

"Hold this for me love," he said. She looked up to see what he wanted her to hold.

"Did I tell you to look up?" His voice was firm, controlled, and it loosed the butterflies in her stomach.

"No Sir. I'm sorry Sir," she whispered.

"Hold this for me," he said offering the cane to her lips.

She opened her mouth and took the cane, holding it in her teeth as she dipped her face back to the mattress fighting the urge to look up at him to gauge whether he was serious or whether this was another version of the familiar game they played. It felt new, different, more…real.

"I'm going to talk. You're going to listen. I'm going to lay out some new rules that are going to govern our relationship from now on. You are not going to say anything but yes Sir or no Sir. Do you understand?"

"Yes Sir," she mumbled around the cane.

"I'm going to do what I should have done years ago and take the time to train you to be the submissive wife that I know you want to be," he said. "You do want to submit to me don't you?" he asked softly.

"Yes Sir," she answered around the cane. They both enjoyed their master/slave game, though she wanted more than a game. She wanted to surrender herself to him completely. She wanted him to master her.

"Full time? 24/7?" he asked.

"Yes Sir." She longed to look up at him, to gauge his expression, to see whether he was seriously laying down a new direction or whether this was part of a game, a fantasy that would leave her disappointed and wishing for more when it ended.

"I've been much too lenient with you, spoiling you instead of giving you the discipline you need, instead of demanding the submission I want."

She could hear him pull a chair up in front of the bed. She could hear the creak as he sat down on it.

"From now on, I'm going to be a demanding bastard," he said, grasping her ponytail and pulling her head up till her gaze met his.

Her stomach clenched, the flood of moisture trickling down her thigh intensified. An empty gaping, wanting feeling filled her chest and spread to her stomach. She wanted what he promised, wanted it badly. If only he would truly hold her to such a high standards.

His expression did not flinch as she looked up at him, the cane still clenched between her teeth. She hoped he was serious, that he wasn't just playing out a fantasy, though she didn't want to give up all of her autonomy. She wanted to maintain some control over her life, her career.

She loved it when he ordered her to do things, or when he merely mentioned that there was something he wanted and left her to get it for him. She loved caring for him, spoiling him. She loved it all the more when it was tied up with his dominance and her submission, when there was an expectation that he would ask and she would submit.

She knew she'd been sloppy in her submission. She called him Master or Sir only when it suited her, begging to be taken out for dinner instead of cooking at home when she knew he preferred to have home cooked meals during the week. She let the laundry pile up in baskets before she put it away. She failed to make the bed. It was true she was busy. She taught several English as a second language classes and preparation for them took a considerable amount of time. Still, she knew deep inside that a part of letting things pile up was the hope that he would notice and demand better of her.

She wasn't happy with herself or the way she kept the house. She wasn't happy with the way she treated him. Yet, without some structure the household chores fell to the wayside and she was sloppy about calling him Master or Sir.

As she knelt on the bed, letting her thoughts rush over her she realized that she needed him to set expectations and to hold her to them. If he did, she would surrender to him, enjoying his power and reveling in her submission. If he didn't there would always be a little something missing…a little something that hung just out of her reach.

"So, love," he said still holding her head up by her hair. "First rule."

She waited wondering what it would be. Wondering whether she'd be able to live up to the expectation, how many times he'd have to spank her before she got it right.

"We need an underlying structure. Something that reminds you that you are my submissive, my wife. That you belong to me. I need something that reminds me of my responsibility to master you, to nurture your natural submission. So, from now on, you *will* call me Master or Sir when we are alone. Dear or by my first name when we are in public."

She liked the sound of it. Master. Sir. She liked the sound of both. They made her feel submissive, mellow, subservient to him. But of the two, she preferred Master. Master implied ownership and power. Sir implied simple respect. Simple submission. She preferred to feel his power, his ownership, to bestow respect and submission because of it but she could live with either name.

She liked the idea of calling him Dear as an equally respectful term of submission and respect when they were in public.

"Dear is just like Master and Sir, a verbal sign of your respect and your submission."

She smiled. Dear. She liked the sound of that. She liked having a vanilla endearment that meant the same as Master or Sir. It would be kind of like a secret code between them. Eventually calling him Dear would make her feel submissive in the same way that calling him Master and Sir did. It would allow them to maintain their roles while their families and friends were oblivious to the undercurrent of respect she bestowed on him and the power and control he exerted over her.

"I am going to be very strict in enforcing this rule. If you speak to me there had dammed well better be a Sir, a Master, or a Dear attached to it. Do I make myself clear?"

"Yes Master," she said softly, feeling herself edge toward that invisible place where she ceded her power to him, where she would derive pleasure from pleasing him.

"Good girl," he said stroking her hair and pushing her face back to the mattress so that once again she couldn't see him.

She fought the urge to arch into his touch, enjoying the gentleness of his touch which was a sharp contrast against the harsh, controlled tone of his voice.

"I am going to keep a count of every omission and I'm going to punish you, severely for each one. I want you to get in the habit of treating me with the respect that a husband, a Master deserves. Do you understand?"

"Yes Sir," she answered around the cane that she still held in her mouth.

"Good girl."

She felt warmed by his praise. Eager to submit, desperate to earn more of his praise.

"There are daily chores that I want you to do, every day. I've been way, way, way too lenient recently and your housekeeping has gotten sloppy. I do not expect you to clean the whole house in the next day or two because we have decided on these new rules. I understand that you have other demands on your time and I want you to be successful with those things. But I do expect you to keep my home clean and in order. There should be nothing more important than our relationship and your service to me. Is that clear?"

He lifted her head again by tugging on her hair. She agreed. There was nothing more important than their relationship and her service to him, though she often acted as if everything else was more important.

She lifted her gaze, meeting his head on. So far she loved the rules he was implementing. They were fair, reasonable, and if she lived up to them she would be a much better submissive than she had ever been. She would become more precise in her submission, less sloppy, and she wanted that. She craved the structure, the order, the expectations and the harsh consequences for not measuring up.

"From now on, I will send you to bed ahead of me. When I send you to bed I want you to prepare yourself for me. You will get into this position on the bed and wait for me. I will expect your eyes to remain downcast unless I tell you that you can look up. When I come in I will ask you about your chores, and whether you have done everything that is required of you. Based upon what you report to me and what I have observed you will receive either punishment or reward or both."

He let her head drop back to the bed, and he stroked the back of her head gently.

"Understand Little One?" he asked.

"Yes Master," she said softly.

"Good girl," he said.

"I expect you to ask to service my cock at least once a day."

She moaned, imagining the pleasure she would have sucking his cock. "Yes Sir," she added.

"I want you to understand that this is not a game Love." He stroked her hair, letting his hand trail down her neck, her shoulders. "I own you Love. Your body, your thoughts, your feelings. Everything you are."

His fingers stroked her back and she moaned softly arching her back to meet his touch, to signal her pleasure. "Yes Master," she mouthed around the cane. She wanted to belong to him…to be owned by him. To have him own her body, her thoughts, her feelings, so that there was nothing he didn't have a right to. She wanted to share it all with him. Just the idea of belonging to him so completely sent shafts of pleasure through her.

"I want you to share a fantasy with me each day. I want to know what excites you. What pleases you. I don't want there to be anything held back." He gripped her hair, lifting her head so that she was forced to meet the steely determination in his gaze. "I intend to be very strict in enforcing this one. You can email your fantasy or you can tell me verbally but before I send you to bed I expect to have heard it. You won't like the consequences if I do not. Do I make myself clear?

"Yes Sir," she answered around the cane, her gaze never leaving his.

"I've put all of this in writing. In kind of a contract between us. I would like you to read it and sign it so that there is no argument later about our responsibilities to each other and the consequences for not living up to them."

Her heart surged. He was serious. He had to be serious.

He'd never asked her to sign a contract agreeing to submit to him before. He had to be taking it more seriously—as more than a game. She felt bubbly, euphoric, as if she'd been granted every wish she'd ever made.

She met his gaze and smiled. "Yes Sir. Happily," she said around the cane.

"Good girl," he said softly, releasing her hair and stroking her cheek. "I want you to understand, there is no going back. If you sign this you will belong to me. I will own you. I will master you. I will nurture you and punish you as I see fit."

She felt as if she was melting inside, as if all of her secret fantasies had been realized.

"Please Sir. This is what I want," she said softly.

"You may sit up so you can read the contract. I'll give you a few minutes to look it over. Then I'll answer any questions you have before you sign."

"Yes Sir! Thank you Sir." Abby said, rolling to a sitting position.

"Don't thank me yet. If you sign these papers, I'm going to cane you, thoroughly, to punish you for your past neglect. We're going to start with a clean slate between us. I'm not planning to go easy on you Love. You need to know I'm serious. The days of leniency are over."

"I will like it. I will love it," she said around the cane.

"Here, I'll take that for now. I'll be using it soon," he said taking the cane from her mouth.

"I'm serious. I'll love it. I have always wanted you to master me full time."

"I know you have love. We'll talk about *how* I know another time." He winked and a shiver passed through her. How did he know so much about her secret desires?

He touched her gently under the chin, lifting her face for his kiss. His mouth settled on hers, a combination of his strength and power and an overwhelming gentleness that made her nipples tingle. His tongue explored the crease of her lips, urging them apart. His hand cradled the back of her head, making her feel safe and protected, warm and nurtured as he kissed her. The trust she felt in him coursed through her leaving her in no doubt that this was what she wanted, what she had always wanted. But how did he know that? She'd never really done more than hint.

She swayed in his embrace, loving the slide of his fingers through her hair as his tongue teased her lips, her mouth, her tongue. She wanted the kiss to go on forever. Wanted his touch to go on forever. Wanted him to hold her like this forever.

When he broke the kiss and stepped away she felt bereft of his strength, his warmth, his power.

"The contract little one..." he said tapping the papers as he laid them on the bed beside her. "When I get back, we'll talk." He winked and stepped out of the bedroom leaving her alone with the contract.

It was so like him to be fair, honorable. Not to push her into something she didn't want. She knew it was important to him for her to know and agree to the new rules he'd set out.

She sat on the bed and studied the contract noticing that he'd not only spelled out her obligations but his as well.

The contract spelled out everything he had talked about and more. It went into detail and described his ownership of her, the requirements he had of her, the consequences for not living up to the requirements.

The contract stipulated hours which she would be allowed to work uninterrupted and other hours when she would be forbidden to work, as the contract stipulated those hours belonged to Master. There were hours that Master owned, but that she could ask permission to work during if she needed extra work time, but the decision would always be Master's. Saturdays and Sundays belonged to Master, but she would be permitted to work if Master was in the office working, or if he were agreeable to her working. Evenings after 7 belonged to Master but she would be allowed to work if Master was working or if she gained his permission. Late evenings, after 9 was Master's time and always belonged to him. She could live with the hours he stipulated, particularly if he gave her permission to work during a few early evenings a week.

The consequences for failing to live up to the rules Master had enacted were harsh and it was clear that Master had thought seriously about how he intended to deal with her bad behavior. Though the contract gave examples which included caning, spanking, orgasm denial, forced orgasms, enemas, and various other tortures the last line in the section on consequences summed it up. Master may employ any means of discipline which does not inflict lasting injury upon slave.

Her heart somersaulted as she read that. Anything? She wondered how fierce his corrections would be. She thought about some of the punishments she'd described on her secret blog and wondered if she'd really want him to inflict those punishments.

The last paragraph of the contract caught her attention and made her heart sink.

If at any point slave believes Master is not living up to his obligations under this contract slave shall immediately express her concerns to Master. If Master agrees that he has failed in his duties as Master, slave shall take over the role of Master and Master shall take over the role of slave for a period of 48 hours.

She didn't want him to fail. She wanted him to succeed. She wanted him to Master her, completely, totally, without reservation.

She stacked the pages of the contract neatly, noticing his signature already scrawled at the bottom.

Master had said he would return. She figured that meant she should wait for him. She sank back into the kneeling position he had put her in when he'd first sent her to the bedroom and waited.

Her stomach did cartwheels and summersaults as she thought about their relationship, all the ways it would change. The completeness of the surrender Master required made her feel nervous, edgy. It made her tingle all over. It made her pussy throb.

She thought about the cane that Master had made her hold earlier, thought about the fiery sting and the welts it would leave in its wake. She wondered how many times Master would strike her, and whether he'd bring her to tears. He'd hinted that he was not going to be lenient on the discipline. She felt sick as she thought about being spanked beyond her endurance, to the point she wanted it to stop. She thought about it going beyond that, being forced to endure Master's discipline until he, not her, decided she'd had enough.

The idea of being truly punished, spanked beyond the point she wanted it to end both scared her and turned her on. It always had. That had been at the core of many of her fantasies for as long as she could remember.

She waited for Master, her stomach feeling jittery and hollow, her pussy tight and hot.

Bryce walked quietly into the bedroom, pleased to see that his submissive wife had returned to her presentation position. She knelt on the bed, her ass raised, her face pressed against her arms, her hands extended slightly in front of her, palms up.

He sucked in a deep breath. He loved seeing her in this position, a position that was so obviously submissive. "Have you finished your reading assignment Love?" he asked stroking his palm lightly over her shoulders and back.

"Yes Master. I've finished," she answered.

"Any questions? Concerns?"

"No, Master. I am ready to sign. I *want* to belong to you. I *want* to serve you. I *want* you to mold me into the best submissive I can be.

His heart softened at her eagerness. She truly was a natural submissive with all the makings of a perfect slave. His heart swelled with pride and love and determination to teach her, mold her, make her shine as a submissive, a slave, a wife.

"Sit up and sign, then we'll take care of your discipline for your recent neglect of your chores and we will start with a clean slate and a new way forward.

She sat up and he handed her a pen. She scrawled her name beneath his, immediately returning to the submissive kneeling position once she'd signed her name.

He smiled at her eagerness. Before he'd stumbled onto her blog he would have thought she'd regret her eagerness after her punishment. He didn't intend to go easy on her, but he wanted her to know he was serious, that he was going to be a lot more demanding than he'd been in the past, that he was going to take her discipline and training much more seriously.

"I think my little slave is eager to begin her servitude," he said, gently stroking her hair, enjoying the softness as it glided through his fingers. She rubbed her head against his palm and moaned.

"Yes Sir, I am eager to start my training. I want to be a better wife and slave."

"You will be a much better wife and slave Love," he said his hand dropping. He picked up the cane and bent it testing its flexibility. "You are a good slave now. You please me very much, except for a few little areas of sloppiness which we are going to cure right now."

She shifted slightly on the bed, as if she was preparing herself to endure the spanking.

"Tell me Abby, what parts of your service to me are you most disappointed in?"

"I don't call you Sir and Master enough." She took a deep breath and let it out. "By not doing that I don't show you the respect you deserve."

"Are you disappointed in yourself about that Love?"

"Yes Master. Very disappointed."

"I am unhappy about that too. The way you address me is the way you show your respect and submission when we are not in a scene. It damages our relationship when you fail to address me properly."

"I know Sir. I am sorry."

"What else Love?"

"The house Sir." Her voice was soft, filled with shame.

He looked around the bedroom at the baskets of laundry, the overflowing hamper, the carpet which needed to be vacuumed, and the unmade bed. Her housekeeping had definitely slipped a lot in the past months. He knew it was a source of irritation for her. It had become a source of irritation to him too.

"Yes, you've fallen behind on your household chores a lot lately. But that's going to change, isn't it Little One?

"Yes Master. I want it to change."

"Do you think you deserve punishment for not addressing me correctly and for getting sloppy with the housework?"

She nodded. Then said so softly he could barely hear her. "Yes Sir, I deserve to be punished."

"Ummm...I agree. I am going to give you the punishment you deserve. Maybe the stripes across your ass will help you focus on your chores and showing me the proper respect."

She shifted on the bed. He could feel the tension and anticipation radiating from her in nearly tangible waves.

"I love you but I am not going to cut you any slack this time. This is a punishment spanking. It *is* going to hurt. A lot." He moved around behind her and ran his hand over the smooth, unblemished cheek of her ass. He knew her ass would not be so smooth and unmarked for quite awhile. He fully expected the next few weeks to be like military boot camp. Grueling. Painful. Difficult for both of them. Her ass would be marked up pretty good for the next few weeks, till she developed the good habits they both wanted her to have.

"You may beg, plead, whimper, whine, cry. I *expect* you to beg and plead and cry, but you're absolutely not to get out of position. I expect you to keep your head down, your eyes closed, and your ass up. If you move out of position, drop your ass, or move your hands to cover your ass or open your eyes, the stroke won't count or we'll start over. Are you ready Love?"

"Yes Master." The words were very soft, almost inaudible.

"You don't have to count the first set. I would like to hear an apology and a thank you after each stroke."

"Yes Master," she said barely above a whisper.

"Close your eyes. Keep them closed," he ordered.

He stepped back, rolled his shoulders and measured the first stroke. He wanted it to land straight across the middle of her ass. Hard.

He drew back and swung. The cane connected right where he'd wanted it to, horizontally, across the middle of her ass. She jerked and yelped. "Owe, owe, owe, God that hurt," she whimpered. She wriggled her ass side to side. He smiled knowing how much she wanted to get out of position, how much she wanted to rub the sting out of the rapidly reddening welt that stretched across her ass. "Oh God Master, I am sorry for not calling you Master and for not keeping the house clean." She sucked in another breath. "But thank you Sir for taking the time to punish me."

He paused a moment, giving her time to anticipate the next stroke, then he measured it, drew back, and struck her hard. The stroke fell right below the first one.

"Owe, owe." She twisted her ass from side to side, but she kept her knees in place and her ass up and her arms beneath her head.

"Good girl. You're doing a nice job of staying in position," he praised, rubbing his hand over the twin welts that crossed her ass.

"Thank you Sir. I'm trying really hard. I'm sorry for the other things. Not calling you master. The house. I really will do better." She let out a deep breath leaned forward and lifted her ass slightly. "Thank you for spanking me Sir."

There was a slight catch in her voice, a little hitch that made his gut tighten and his cock swell. He loved the submission. Loved her surrendering herself to him in this way, loved the trust that she was placing in him.

"Ready love?" he asked measuring the next stroke.

"Yes Master."

The cane struck hard just above the other two welts leaving a bright red line in its wake.

"Oh God, I'll be good. I promise I will call you Master and Sir and I'll clean the house."

She shifted her ass side to side and he knew she longed to reach back and rub the sting away.

"You're fighting me love," he said softly. "Stop fighting against the spanking and my power and surrender to it. The longer you fight me the longer we'll be here. I can stand here and do this all night."

"I am surrendering Sir. I've not moved out of position. I'm obeying."

"Yes, Love, but you're fighting your own desire to surrender your power totally to me. You're still holding onto that little bit of control trying to get me to stop spanking you by promising you'll be good rather than admitting you deserve this spanking."

The words spun around in Abby's mind. She didn't fully comprehend the distinction. She was surrendering to him. She was kneeling ass up. He was striping her ass with the cane. What more did he want?

"I'm sorry Sir. I've been sloppy in my submission to you," she said. Thank you for taking me in hand. I know being spanked will make me a better wife…a better slave. But God… it REALLY hurts Sir."

"I know it hurts Love. It's supposed to hurt. Are you ready for the next one?"

"Please Sir…" she wasn't sure whether she was begging for the next stroke or for leniency. The stroke fell like a sizzling stripe of fire across her ass. She screamed and would have reached back to rub her ass if Master's voice hadn't broken through the red haze of pain that filled her mind.

"Don't even think about breaking position," he warned.

"It hurts!"

"Surrender Love. You're still fighting me. Do you deserve the spanking?"Yes," she whimpered.

"Then accept the punishment…surrender to it."

"I am submitting! You are fucking spanking me and it fucking hurts like a son of a bitch. What more do you want?"

"Fucking? Son of a bitch?" He chuckled. "It's good to know I have your undivided attention."

Unreasonable anger shot through her. She'd wanted this, asked for this. But she hadn't expected him to strike her so hard, for it to hurt so much. She felt like she had gashes in her ass.

"Deep breath Love." He waited while she took a deep breath and let it out. "Tell me again how sorry you are."

Frustration coiled within her. She was sorry, but she felt frustrated, unsure what he wanted from her. He kept saying he wanted her surrender, but she was surrendering.

"I am sorry Sir. I've not been a very good wife for quite a long time. Thank you for taking time to spank me."

"Good Girl," he said. She felt the warm, confident stroke of his hand as it ran over the welts on her ass.

"Ready Love?"

"Yes. Sir." She gritted her teeth and dipped her chin. God, she wanted him to stop. She wanted it to end. She didn't know how much longer she could maintain control if he kept spanking her like this, so measured, so hard, with so much damned control.

The next stroke stung licking across her ass like a liquid, throbbing fire. She yelped and jerked. If anything this stroke had been harder than the last. She couldn't endure another stroke like it. It hurt too much.

"God Sir, I'm sorry. I'll be good from now on. Please. Stop. It hurts." Her voice had taken on a desperate tone. She wanted to open her eyes, meet his gaze, beg him to stop till he complied.

"No Love, for once, we're going to break through this stubbornness. I am going to continue to spank you till you surrender completely to me."

"I don't know how to surrender any more completely." The frustration she felt laced her voice.

"For a start, stop trying to convince me to stop spanking you and accept that it is my right to spank you as hard and for as long as I think you need it. Stop fighting against the pain and accept it."

She struggled to wrap her mind around the idea of not fighting against the pain. If she didn't fight the pain she would melt into an undignified pile of weeping mess. It was only the tight control that she maintained that kept that from happening.

"Thank me and prepare for the next stroke Love."

She swallowed hard. She clenched her jaw, determined not to cry out when the fiery wrath of the stroke sliced across her ass.

"Thank you Sir for punishing me. I want you to punish me for my misdeeds."

"Then stop fighting it," he whispered stroking her cheek. I expect you to cry, to shed real tears. The longer you fight them the longer the spanking will continue."

He wanted her to cry? She didn't know if she could. She'd never cried from a spanking, even when she'd been a kid. Even back then she'd realized that if she remained stoic in the face of pain she maintained her power. She'd never wanted to give her father power over her so she'd endured the strokes of his belt without tears.

But she didn't want to maintain power now. She wanted to give her power to Master. She wanted to surrender completely to him.

"Ready Love?" His voice was calm, controlled, there was no anger or malice. Just calm, control. The tone of calm, of control, made her feel safe, cared for. So unlike the spankings of her childhood when spankings had been out of control, crazy events.

"Yes, Master, I am ready," she said thinking that maybe she really was ready. Maybe she really was ready to surrender everything…her past, her present, her future, to Master.

The stroke streaked across her ass searing her flesh. But something changed in her. She lifted her hips higher, accepting the pain, taking it, surrendering herself to it.

"Thank you Master. I am sorry I've not shown you the proper respect."

Bryce noticed the change in her. It was like all the energy she had used to maintain control, to fight against the pain had melted and in its place was peace, serenity.

"Good Girl," he said stroking his palm down her back to her hips. He wanted to push his fingers into her hot, wet cunt, but knew there would be time for that later. First he needed to claim the gift she had given him. She'd finally submitted fully. It was time he claimed the gift.

"Ready Love?"

"Yes Master," she answered. Her voice sounded peaceful, content. She was not begging him to stop, was not telling him how much it hurt. Instead she lifted her hips.

When the lash fell hard against the lower cheek of her ass she sucked in a deep breath. He saw the tears seep from her eyes.

"Another Love." His voice was firm. Calm. Controlled.

The next stroke fell on her upper thighs, just beneath the last one. The tears trickled from her closed eyes.

"Another Love." This stroke landed solidly just beneath the last. Her breath shuddered in her chest and the tears continued to flow.

"That's my good girl. Let it go. Give it all to me."

"I'm sorry I was such a brat all these years Master. Thank you for making me see it."

With that she lifted her ass. "Another please, Sir"

He complied, letting five or six more fall in rapid succession. When she was sobbing loudly, her face covered in tears he said, "Last five Love. Count them for me."

She surrendered completely as she counted out the last five of the strokes. Master was not gentle with the last five. It was as if he was using them to draw out her submission.

Her ass throbbed, the wicked welts made her feel as if there were heavy gashes from the top of her ass cheeks to midway down the backs of her thighs, but she didn't care. Master would take care of the welts. His touch would soothe them, make them better.

The spanking had cleared the air not just between her and Master. The spanking had made her realize that though she tried not to be controlling, she had never really left behind the events of her childhood and had diligently fought Master for control, even at those times she most wanted to submit.

The spanking had shown them a new way forward into a future where she would submit wholeheartedly without reservation and Master would own her submission as the precious gift that it was.

Starla Kaye

Trusting Her

Sam Caldwell looked down at the cup of coffee slowly growing cold in front of him. Growing cold, like his marriage of late. It was his own damn fault, too. He used to be able to handle everything pretty much on his own. Well, with his handful of reliable ranch hands who he guided along with little or no instruction most of the time. They knew what to do, and he trusted them to do their jobs. But he was the man in charge around the Circle C.

He took a sip of the cool coffee and grimaced. Should have taken a drink sooner. He shouldn't have spent all this time sitting here fretting about the problems in his life like some old woman. Instead he should have more than half-listened to two of the neighboring ranchers with him in the booth of the town's favorite diner.

Saturday mornings generally had him sitting here chatting and bs-ing with a few of the ranchers in the area. This was their time to catch up on not only what was going on with their ranches but also with the sad state of affairs for ranchers in general. He usually chimed in with his opinions.

But today he hadn't said much. He wasn't even all that interested in what was being said. His thoughts kept wandering back to how his wife had stopped smiling around him lately, how she had begun keeping her distance from him. Truth was, his ranch hands were starting to avoid him as well.

"When you going to snap out of this blue funk you've been in?" Pete asked from across the table. "You've been grouchier than a wounded bear the last month."

His other friend nodded agreement. "You and Katie aren't having problems, are you? I'd sure hate to hear that."

Were they? No, he was the problem. Sam shook his head and abandoned holding onto the cold cup of coffee. He offered a weak excuse for his behavior of late. "If a man had a snippy time of the month like a woman does, then I guess that's what's happening with me. Hell, even I can't stand to be around me right now." That was the truth, too.

His friends chortled and took off talking about the horrors of dealing with their wives when they were PMS-ing. Sam wasn't up to listening to that. He stood to dig coffee money out of his jeans' pocket and set it on the table. They went right on with the current subject of their conversation, how Pete's wife turned into Dragon Woman once a month. Sam counted himself lucky in that moment. His Katie got a little testy at that time of the month, and sometimes he even had to warm her backside to straighten her out, but, all in all, it wasn't so bad.

He grabbed his Stetson from a hook on the wall beside the table and planted it on his head. "See you next week, boys."

"Kiss that sweet wife of yours, let some of her cheery disposition rub off on you," Pete teased as Sam walked through the half-full diner toward the door.

He caught a few more comments about his sour mood of late from some of the other ranchers hanging around and drinking coffee. One man even called out that he needed a swift kick in the butt or something. If he didn't know that the men taunting him actually liked him, he might have stopped to snap at them. But he managed to take their ribbing in stride and headed out to his pickup truck. If he wasn't in a better mood by next week, even his old friends might start steering clear of him. He needed to work through whatever had him going around in a crotchety mood, complaining when there wasn't anything to complain about, snapping at others for no reason. Especially at his wife.

By the time he pulled onto the gravel road leading to his ranch, the sun was high in the sky. It promised to be a real burner for late in May, but then this was Kansas. It could be a burner one day and plumb cold the next this time of year. All you could really count on was the wind, which never seemed to stop. But, as he drove past the heart of the ranch buildings and to his driveway, it wasn't the heat of the day that had him feeling cantankerous and sweaty. No, it was the strange turn of thoughts he'd been mulling over for the last few miles. Really strange. Never would he have imagined himself thinking along this line.

Spanking. He never really gave it much thought except when it was necessary that he turn his wife over his knee for a sound walloping. She had a tendency to get over-tired and then cranky, so he burned her bottom to get her refocused. Sometimes she failed to follow through on a promise she made to him or to one of the community groups she was involved with, so he heated her backside for letting whoever it was down. He'd been spanking her, with her acceptance, since before they'd married. After a spanking her attitude definitely improved, even if she might not sit well for a day or two. The fact that he spanked her for discipline wasn't an issue between them. He loved her and she knew it, even when he reddened her butt.

He pulled into the driveway and turned off the engine. It really hadn't been spanking Katie that he'd been thinking about these final miles. He gripped the steering wheel for a second to rein in his thoughts again. *Can I really do it? Can*

I humble myself enough to tell Katie I need a spanking?

His buttocks clenched just at the idea. Did Katie's bottom clench like this when he told her he was going to spank her? He remembered how she usually sucked in a nervous breath and the way her eyes widened in distress and her pretty cheeks turned pink when he brought up the subject. It wasn't a pleasant subject for either of them, or a pleasant experience. But she took her punishment, sometimes with a bit of resistance at first or a weak attempt at protesting. It came back to her knowing he loved her and her trusting him.

He let go of the steering wheel and pressed his lips together in grim determination. Hell, he knew she loved him. And he certainly trusted her. So he damn well needed to stop pondering this issue and just do something about it. A spanking helped his wife when she had attitude problems, so surely it would help him, too.

Determined and a bit anxious about his crazy notion, he got out of his truck. His heart raced, and he took a second to steady his emotions. He stood staring at the log home he and his men had built five years ago. It made him proud to look at it, especially knowing how much Katie loved the place. He'd built it with proposing to her in mind. He'd been in love with her ever since high school when she'd first brought him to his knees with a simple kiss. They'd dated off and on while he went to college at Kansas State University and she went to the University of Kansas. Being separated like that hadn't made a relationship easy.

Fact was, relationships were never easy. There had been a time when he'd thought she was drifting away from him, and probably should have because he'd been somewhat of an idiot.

He'd failed them both and gone out one lonely night with one of the cheerleaders. Katie had been spitting mad when he'd guiltily admitted it. She'd gotten so pissed at him, so out of control, that he'd finally bent her over his knee for the first time and spanked the sass right out of her. She'd not spoken to him for two weeks after that. Then she'd come to the frat house where he'd been living and flat out told him they were getting married as soon as they graduated.

He looked toward the kitchen where he was pretty certain she'd be baking something for him. She loved to bake, and she spoiled him and his men something awful. Every one of them had a sweet tooth. No doubt about it, he was a damn lucky man. Lately, though, he knew he wasn't any kind of prize husband-wise. And she sure didn't deserve his sour attitude.

He sucked in a deep breath and bucked up his courage. Maybe when he told her about this one crazy idea she'd run fleeing from the insane man he'd become. But what if she didn't? What if she went along with this wild notion? Could he actually go through with it?

Set one damn foot in front of another and get your sorry ass in the house. Go talk to your wife. Trust in her. All of that was a hell of a lot easier said than done.

Yet he forced his legs to move and turned his back to the rest of the ranch, knowing that there were a lot of chores he should be helping with instead of doing this. But if he chickened out and turned around now, he knew he'd never round up the nerve to do this again. *Just keep walking. The chores will get done without you today. You need this.*

Katie hummed along to the country music coming from the radio on the counter across the kitchen. Her heart wasn't actually into the music, though. She'd been worried about Sam when he sped out of the ranch yard this morning on his way into Haverty to have the usual Saturday morning coffee with his buddies. Actually, she'd been worried about him for a while now. He'd gotten this surly and stayed that way for this long one other time in the six years that they'd been married. She'd almost considered leaving him then. She wouldn't consider it this time, she loved him too much. She just needed to find out how to help him out of this mood. If only he'd talk to her about what was bothering him. If only she knew how to ask him about it, without having him snap at her.

She had decided to bake him an apple pie, his favorite dessert. The timer went off on the stove at the same time she heard the familiar sound of Sam's heavy footsteps headed in her direction. Uneasiness flitted through her. The need for her husband to walk into the room, pull her to him, and kiss her silly also filled her. But she doubted that would happen today. It hadn't happened in too long.

She pulled the sizzling pie from the oven as he walked into the kitchen. She heard his appreciative deep inhale of the spicy scent and the way his stomach rumbled. He'd refused breakfast before he'd left for town. It sounded like he hadn't eaten at the diner either.

"Something wrong?" she asked warily, setting the pie on a hot pad on the counter. She knew that he wasn't around the house this time of day, except on Sundays for their usual big noon feast with the ranch hands. She couldn't imagine what had brought him here now, unless…. No, it couldn't be for that reason. She'd been on her best behavior lately.

He met her gaze, looking even more serious than normal. It took him a few seconds, but he finally blurted out, "I need your help with something."

Katie gaped at him, confused. She could count on one hand the number of times he'd asked her for help since they'd said their I-dos. "Sure, of course." She tried to study his expression, but he was even harder to read than usual. "Does this have anything to do with how… with how…well, with how disgruntled you've been lately? With what's bothering you?"

Sam took off his hat and set it brim up on the counter. "Disgruntled, huh? Don't you mean acting like an ass?"

Her blue eyes widened at his bluntness. "You have been a little out of sorts." *Okay, serious understatement.* He'd become almost unbearable to live with.

He leaned against the counter and seemed to struggle with what to say next. His handsome face pinched in frustration until he said, "When you get all grumpy and out of sorts, you get your sweet butt burned."

As always happened when they talked in any way about spanking, her cheeks flamed in acknowledgment. She was a spanked wife, as embarrassing as that was, but she accepted it because she loved her big cowboy husband far more than she disliked being spanked.

He held her gaze and she knew that he, too, was remembering how only a couple of days ago she'd gone over his knee and he'd spanked her bottom until it turned good and red. Not that that was unusual. He spanked her fairly regularly. She tended to get mouthy at times, had a bit more of a temper control problem than he liked, and she could be a little more independent and rebellious than he tolerated. She hated getting spanked at the time, but she easily forgave him when they had their make-up sex later.

Uncomfortable with his continued silence and frown, she pulled the oven mitts from her hand and nervously said, "I haven't done..." She didn't finish the thought, knowing he would understand anyway.

"No, darlin', I'm not here to talk about burning your butt again."

Thank goodness. The tension eased out of her. "Okay, so why are you here? What do you want me to help you with?"

He stood there looking at her as if he didn't know how to continue, as if he wished he'd never walked into the kitchen. She wasn't used to him being this indecisive. She was used to the man who kindly but firmly controlled everything on the ranch and in his household. When she was in trouble, she knew it real fast. He didn't waste much time with lecturing her on the whys. He took her over his knee or bent her over something and fired up her poor bottom. Likewise, when he was in the mood for sex, he didn't waste a lot of time...unless he was in the mood for spending some long, serious time taking her from one orgasm to another. Usually he got right down to business and took her quick and hard. Generally speaking, that was good for her, too.

"Sam, what's going on here? Speak to me."

He thrust his chin out, straightened his shoulders, and stated grimly, "I need you to help me with my attitude problem."

She blinked. "I don't understand."

His expression mirrored frustration. He shifted awkwardly. "What happens when you have attitude issues?"

Katie felt quivers of knowledge in her stomach. Her buttocks tingled in memory. Her cheeks grew heated again, and she said quietly, "You spank me."

"Bingo!" He looked almost joyous that she understood.

She still didn't fully comprehend what he was getting at. "You want *me* to spank you?" Surely she was misunderstanding him.

He glanced away, and she watched color creep up his face. Embarrassed?

"I don't really *want* to be spanked, no," he admitted and she felt relieved. "I need it, though, like you do sometimes. At least I think I do."

"I don't ever *need* to be spanked," she automatically protested, stopping when he raised one eyebrow in challenge.

He let her comment go and studied the scuffed toes of his boots. "Hell, Katie, I don't really know anything except I can't keep going around growling and snapping at everyone. Including you." He looked up, and she saw his incredible love for her in his eyes. "Especially you."

That roundabout apology warmed her. He didn't say he was sorry easily. This had to be tough on him, this humbling himself to come to her with this bizarre request. She chewed her lower lip for a second and finally said, "I'm not sure I can do it, spank you. It even sounds strange. I get spanked, not you."

"Until now." His jaw was set in determination, although his eyes hinted at his wariness.

It was so hard for her to comprehend what he wanted done. *Spanked. He wants me to spank him.* He would never want any of his ranch hands or his friends finding out about this, just as she preferred her being a spanked wife kept private. He was pure Alpha male, dominant, a leader, the head of his house. He turned her over his knee and reddened her bottom when he felt she needed it, not that she'd ever really fought him about it. This talk about punishing him was well beyond "thinking out of the box," as far as she was concerned.

"You love me, right?"

"Of course I do! Maybe you've pushed my nerves lately, but I love you anyway." She knew he wanted an answer, but she couldn't give him one right now. "I need to think, Sam. You can't just spring something like this on me."

Disappointment crossed his face, but he nodded. "I reckon you're right. It boggles my mind a bit thinking about it, too."

"Why don't you go wait in our bedroom while I consider the matter?" The second the question was out of her mouth she wondered if she'd gone too far. She'd been the one sent to their bedroom in the past.

That eyebrow went up again, but he calmly said, "I suppose it's only right that I be sent upstairs to await my fate."

"Like you make me do sometimes. When I have to go fret over what you're going to do: spank me with your hand, thrash me with your belt, or whale at me with the paddle." She nodded and gave a weak smile.

"Yes, I guess it's your turn to deal with the whole unpleasant waiting time. Even if I decide that I can't do as you asked." Actually, she kind of liked the idea of sending him to their bedroom to think about being punished. A taste of his own medicine.

"Now that I'm facing this waiting time, I don't really like it. I'm pretty sure you don't like it, either." He heaved a sigh and turned to walk back out of the room. "Am I going to have to wait long?"

He usually made her wait at least a half hour, maybe longer. It was really tempting to let him stew for a good long while, but, as impatient as he could be at times, he was going to get frustrated really fast. "I'll be up in a half hour."

Katie watched her big cowboy husband walk out of the kitchen. Surprised didn't come close to how she felt. Stunned was more like it. Her heart raced at the strange idea. He had a good hundred pounds on her and a good ten inches. He'd crush her if she took him over her knee for a spanking.

Spank him? He wants me to spank him? She slumped against the counter and looked at the apple pie she'd baked him in the hope that his favorite dessert would bring him out of his sour mood. But it wasn't a pie he wanted. He wanted her to spank him. She just couldn't wrap her mind around the concept.

Still... He had been making everyone—including her— walk on eggshells lately, afraid they'd cross him wrong and get a verbal lashing for no good reason. He hadn't been kissing her, hugging her, or paying her much attention in bed either lately. She certainly missed their normal intimacy. Maybe he really did need a good shaking up, a stern talking to. A spanking.

Her gaze shifted to the pantry where the worn paddle he used at least every couple of months on her poor bottom hung on a hook. Gawd, she hated that paddle. It stung like the dickens, but it taught quite a lesson, too. She sure didn't misbehave in that particular way again anytime soon. If she was going to spank him, the paddle would probably be the best choice. Her small hand sure wouldn't deliver much of a punishment.

Still, could she actually do this? Spank the man who had always been the head of their household, who corrected her misbehavior, who soundly punished her when she broke one of their rules? He was a leader amongst the ranching community. He wore confidence and authority so easily. He gave an order and his men didn't even question it. How could such a man humble himself to let her—to ask her—to spank him?

When he'd walked in the door in the middle of the day, she'd been immediately concerned. She'd started going through everything she'd done in the last few days, trying to determine if he'd shown up out of the blue to punish her for something. And she'd vividly recalled how he'd spanked her the other day for acting sassy about.... In truth, she couldn't even remember now what she'd acted sassy about. It didn't matter. Once he spanked her all was forgiven.

She dug the mixing bowl and beaters out of the sink to put them in the dishwasher. Her gaze landed on the rubber spatula, which made her think about the hard, wide wooden spoon in the drawer. Her buttocks clenched. More than a few times Sam had pulled it from the drawer and given her a few sharp whacks with that nasty spoon. Should she use the spoon on his bare bottom? Let him have that "wonderful" experience?

Okay, she'd obviously decided that she would do as he asked, since she was now playing around in her mind with what implement she'd use. Her stomach fluttered with nerves not unlike it did when she was the one sent to their bedroom to await punishment. She hated waiting. And she loved her husband enough not to make him wait any longer for her decision.

Determined to do as he asked of her, she went to the pantry and took down the paddle. It was the first time she carried it not because he'd told her to bring it to him, but because she was going to use it *on* him. Her fingers tingled at even holding the paddle. It felt cool to her touch, but she knew from experience it soon turned an equally cool bottom hot.

Walking away from his wife, walking up the stairs and to their bedroom to await her decision had been damn hard. Sam toed off his boots and began pacing the bedroom. What would she decide? At least she hadn't looked at him like he'd become insane. She'd looked shocked, yes, but justifiably so. His idea had shocked him as well, still did. But he would stand behind it and accept whatever choice she made.

He glanced out the window to see several of his ranch hands getting ready to ride out on horseback to do some checking on the cattle in the west field. Normally he'd be riding out with them. Instead he was in this room waiting to find out if his sweet wife loved him enough to spank his ass. *Spank him!* It sounded so odd. He hadn't been turned over someone's knee and had his butt beat in nearly twenty years. And he'd never been spanked by a woman, not even his mother. Could he really do this?

Finally he heard Katie's footsteps coming up the stairs. Thank goodness! He didn't think he could have withstood waiting any longer. He might have to rethink how long he made her wait for punishment in the future.

He tensed and turned to watch her walk into the bedroom. His stomach knotted as he spotted the worn, foot-long wooden paddle from the pantry in her hand. This could be bad. He remembered her crying hard when he gave her a good, firm paddling. Sometimes she even screamed. He was tough, he would keep it together.

"I guess you've made your decision. You're going to punish me." He stood by the window and noted how her shoulders were stiff. Her chin set with determination.

"I decided you wouldn't have asked me to do this if it wasn't really important to you." She moved further into the room, her small hand holding tight to the paddle. "If it's so important to you, then it is to me as well."

He couldn't seem to stop looking at the paddle, much as he remembered her doing before he applied it to her bottom. "I'm hoping it'll improve my attitude, like it tends to do yours. I'm tired of everyone avoiding me. Of being irritated with myself." He walked around the bed and waited for instruction.

"If we're being honest here, then I'll tell you that I'm real tired of your grouching around, too. And I'm even more tired of you coming to bed in a sour mood, turning away from me, and going to sleep without even a goodnight kiss." Her mouth pursed in annoyance at that admission.

Guilt weighed on him. She was right. "I'm sorry, sweetheart."

Her chin ratcheted up a notch. "As you tell me, 'sorry' is an easy word to say, especially when facing a spanking. Meaning it isn't quite so easy." She glanced at the pillows. "Stack a couple of them on the end of the bed. Then you can take those jeans off before you bend over the pillows."

Sam went to get the pillows, thinking about how many dozens of times he'd made her do this little pre-spanking chore. It wasn't easy to do when you knew you'd soon be stretched over them with your butt in the air waiting to be swatted. But he did it, and he pulled off his jeans and tossed them aside. At her simple nod, he drew in a breath and stretched over the pillows. It felt really odd to be in this position, vulnerable. She was in charge now, not him. His gut knotted. It was damn hard to give up being in charge.

She walked next to him and gently folded his shirt tail onto his back, his tighty-whities still covered his butt. Again, he thought about how he sometimes put her in this position, with her panties still on. Sometimes he made her strip completely first. He was glad she hadn't made him do that. This was humiliating enough.

Then with an amazing show of strength, she landed the paddle with a biting Swat! His eyes flashed wide and he gasped, "Shit!"

"The first one is always the worst." She reached down to smooth the sting as he sometimes did. "Now, shall I lecture you about why you're getting spanked? Like you do me."

"I'd just as soon not." He didn't like being in this position now that he was actually here.

She sent another smack to his other butt cheek. "Exactly how I feel when bent over with my bottom up for your undivided attention. That doesn't stop you from reciting everything I've done wrong and why I'm going to get a sound spanking."

He had a feeling she was starting to enjoy this situation. Payback really could be a bitch.

The smooth wood of the paddle settled against his smarting butt and she said, "Okay, let's go over the reasons why you find yourself bent over the bed just now."

Whack! "You've been growling around the ranch for nearly a month."

Whack! "You've been biting my head off for no good reason, otherwise barely even talking to me." Whack!

Sam hissed, "Damn, sweetheart, lighten up a bit."

"Lighten up? Are you kidding me? We've barely even started and you're wussing already!" Clearly annoyed, she nailed his butt hard a dozen times, alternating between cheeks.

He could barely catch his breath. *Shit, shit, shit!*

"Now, where was I?"

Sam glanced awkwardly back and found her standing beside him, holding the paddle. His butt stung like the devil already. "How about you forget the lecturing and just finish up?"

The look she gave him told him he should have kept his mouth shut. She raised the paddle and he turned his head away a second before the hard wood connected with his butt again with a room-echoing whack!

"Shit!" he barked and curled his hands into the quilt.

"Got your attention again, I take it." She smoothed a hand over his blazing bottom. "Heating up nicely."

How many times had he said that to her during a spanking? Too many.

"Okay, one more reason why you're getting spanked and then I'll 'just finish up,' as you suggested." Whack! "Other than make-up sex after you spank me, we haven't had hot and sweaty sex in months." Whack! "And I'm really, really upset about that."

"Katie, I'm sorry," he gritted out. He was, too. "I've been an idiot."

"As you so often say, 'damn right.'"

He started to push up. "I'll get my head on straight. No more grouching around. No more..."

She shoved him back down. "Uh-uh. Not done yet." She went back to turning his ass into a mound of pain. Swat after swat blasted against his butt, never letting up, covering every inch. She must have given him at least a couple dozen whacks with that god-awful paddle.

One sharp whack shot him deeper into the pillows, had him yelling out, "Katie! Stop! Enough!" He sucked in a ragged breath, tears stung his eyes. "I'm sorry as hell. For everything. I'll take you right now. I swear, I'll do anything you want. Just stop."

Sam curled his fingers tighter on the quilt. His teeth were gritted together so hard his jaw hurt. Why the hell had he asked for this? How the hell did she endure it time and time again? His respect for her grew even more.

"So you're truly sorry for your misbehavior? Not just tired of getting your bottom paddled?" She held the wood against his lower cheeks. She questioned him just as he did her, testing to see if he'd had enough. She would stop, he knew that.

If she could take a firmer paddling than this, he sure could. Macho fool that he was. "Do I stop paddling your butt with your first pleas and promises?"

The paddle lifted and she sighed. "No. You paddle me until I'm wriggling all over the pillows. Until my legs are kicking up and I'm swearing on my life never to misbehave again. Sometimes until I'm sobbing my heart out."

He sure didn't want to do any of that, but he couldn't show weakness yet. He was tougher than she was. "Then I guess you'd better start swinging that paddle again."

To his surprise she set the paddle on the bed next to him. Then she said, "It's time I pulled these shorts down and bared that bottom of yours."

Bared his bottom! Sure, he did that to her, should have expected this was coming. But hell! His face heated. This was damn embarrassing. It took all his inner control to stay in position over the pillows and raise up on his toes enough that she could tug his undershorts down to his knees. He looked straight ahead at the headboard. His face flamed almost as much as his ass at the humiliation of what she'd done, of his vulnerability. He never thought anything of doing this to her. A spanking was best delivered on the bare.

She picked up the paddle and repeated what he'd told her many times. "The most memorable spankings are delivered to a bare butt, or so I'm told on a regular basis." She leaned down to kiss one burning ass cheek. "Pretty embarrassing, isn't it?"

"I have to admit it is. It doesn't mean I won't still be doing it to you in future spanking sessions." But he'd appreciate her acceptance of his insistence on doing so more next time.

The loud Whack! of the paddle shot him forward into the pillows and had him sucking in a breath. He guessed she didn't like him talking about "future spanking sessions."

"Hold on tight, cowboy. I'm getting ready to make sure you don't sit well in the saddle or anywhere else for at least a day." She rained a quick shower of swats that proved she was serious.

"Damn, woman!" he bit out, curling his toes into the carpet.

The swats kept right on coming until she said, "My arm is getting tired."

"My ass is near worn out." He was more than ready for her to stop.

But she didn't, she evidently found a new source of strength because she went back to blazing up the fire already flaming on his ass. "I'm doing this until you tell me to stop. Or until I think you've had enough."

Tell her to stop! Do it! You won't sit for a week if she keeps this up. Idiot that he was, he refused to break so easily. *Easily?* He remained silent, except for panting between swats.

Then it happened, to his horror. He kicked a leg up at the knee, then stomped down hard at the miserable pain from one particularly hard swat.

He didn't quit a spanking, though, just because she kicked her legs. She wasn't broken at that point. And they'd both agreed years ago that if he was going to spank her, he would do it until she'd taken all she could. She needed to learn whatever lesson was being taught well enough that she couldn't fail it again for a long time. She didn't give up on him now either.

The damn paddle kept right on landing against his throbbing butt. Finally he blinked back a tear, again to his horror. Then he felt one trickle down his face at the same time he shot forward and deep into the pillows, yelling out, "Okay! Stop! Dammit, stop!"

He sensed the paddle still held up in the air and he vowed painfully, "I'll apologize to everyone on the ranch if that's what you want. I'll make love to you three times a day. Anything! Just stop!"

To his relief, Katie immediately backed away. She didn't say a word for several seconds. He couldn't talk anyway. Holy Hell he hurt!

"You should probably stay there for a while longer," she said, sounding uncertain about telling him that.

Now that she'd done as he'd asked, as he'd practically begged her to do, she seemed worried about his reaction. Truth was, he didn't really look forward to getting up at the moment. Not that he liked lying in this embarrassing position with his red ass on display. Again, that made him realize all that he asked of her when he paddled her sweet butt.

He closed his eyes and blinked away the remaining moisture in them. He sure didn't want her seeing tears. "How long do you want me to stay here?" he asked, trying to let her know that she was still in charge and that he was okay with it. But he really just wanted her to leave him be for a bit so he could come to terms with the fierce pain.

"Ummm, ten minutes?" She remained hesitant.

"Yeah thirty minutes sounds about right." He didn't think he'd be able to pull his darn jeans on any sooner than that. His butt felt swollen, every freaking inch of it.

"Well, okay." He heard her moving toward the doorway, but she stopped to add, "I think this is where I'm supposed to tell you that you're forgiven for your bad behavior."

Sam tried to crane his head around to look at her and even that small movement had him flinching. Shit. Yet he found the grace to say, "This is where I tell you how sorry I am. And I am, darlin', real sorry."

Her gaze was focused on his naked rear propped up in the air, red and throbbing. He knew exactly what she was seeing. She gave him a gentle smile, one filled with so much love that it humbled him even more than getting soundly paddled.

"Not pretty, is it? You've got a wicked arm on you, Katie." In spite of his pain, he was damn proud of her. He knew she hadn't wanted to do this, but she'd done it anyway. He wasn't sure he'd ever want to go through this again, but, he supposed, time would tell.

Katie's smile turned up a notch and tipped at the edge with amusement. "It's kind of nice to be on the other side of this spanking thing. Besides, you've deserved a good paddling for a while now."

He shifted slightly once more and groaned before he could control it. Her smile disappeared, and she started toward him, but he shook his head. "No, not yet. No comforting just yet. I need to have some time alone to deal with what happened."

She stopped, looking at him in understanding. "Pretty tough on your supreme machoness, wasn't it? Bruised your ego a little. But you'll get beyond this pain. I'm sure in no time at all you'll be back to strutting around here like the Super Stud you are."

Sam gave her a wobbly grin. "Hard to feel all 'supreme macho' after having been soundly paddled by my loving wife. Or like 'Super Stud' with my ass on fire and sticking up in the air." Still, his cock was starting to perk to life from where it was pressed into the pillows. "I might not be able to fully earn the title of 'Super Stud' until tonight, darlin'."

The plump breasts he so loved to caress and suckle rose and fell in her growing arousal. Her eyes heated. "Looking forward to it, cowboy."

She pulled the bedroom door closed with a final, "I'll let you alone now to pout in private."

"I'm not going to pout," he countered. He collapsed against the pillows and heaved a shuddery sigh. Getting spanked was not easy to deal with. No sir, his ass was in pure misery.

* * * *

Katie had been keeping herself busy in the kitchen, trying to come to terms with what she'd done to Sam. She'd actually spanked him. It still seemed surreal, but her arm hurt from swinging the paddle so long. Did his arm ever hurt after spanking or paddling her?

She thought about how red his bottom had been when she'd stopped. It had to hurt, a lot. *Been there, had that bottom.* She sympathized, somewhat. In truth, he'd deserved the spanking, and she was pleased that she'd had the nerve to actually give it to him. But now she was worried about him. She didn't like for anyone to suffer, and he would, even if he wouldn't admit it. He had chores to get to yet today. No, it wouldn't be any fun at all doing his chores and having his jeans rubbing against his tender bottom.

She was so lost in thought that she didn't hear her husband come into the room. When his hands settled on her shoulders as she looked out the kitchen window, she jumped. "You startled me. I thought you were still upstairs."

"Finished my spell of pouting." He lifted her hair to nuzzle her neck. "Thought maybe I should start following through with my promises. Like making love to my wife."

His kissing her neck always made her weak in the knees. She sighed. "Your chores…"

He rubbed against her from behind, nudging between her legs with his very hard, very long cock. "Chores can wait. You're more important, and I've been neglecting you. Gotta make up for that now."

She turned in his arms and snuggled into him, pleased that he was now naked from head to toe. With a sassy grin, she reached around to put her hands on his bottom. "Naughty boy got his butt spanked. It's still warm."

He grinned down at her. "Still sore as hell, too." Then he took her hand to tug her with him. "Naughty boy wants to take his naughtiness to a whole new level. You up for that?"

Katie laughed, heart racing. "If this is how you're going to act after a spanking, I just might have to do it more often."

"I'm hoping it won't have to happen very often." He pulled her faster toward the bedroom.She hesitated and he stopped to look back at her. "So you'd let me spank you again?" It still amazed her.

His expression turned serious. "I love you, sweetheart. I burn your bottom when I think you need it. Guess it wouldn't be right if I didn't accept a spanking from you now and then."

She smiled and then kissed him. "Make-up sex. Now!"

Starla Kaye

Testing Their Love

From the middle of their rumpled bed, BJ watched Grayson adjust his tie to the perfect Windsor knot. His Ralph Lauren dress shirt, the Black Label tailored suit, all the way to his Innsbrook loafers were flawless. Even his dark hair feathered with gray was stylishly cut and every hair lay in place. Beneath his clothes was a well-toned body. If ever a man fit the image of GQ perfection, he did. But this wasn't the side of him she preferred.

Barely able to move even a muscle, she inhaled the scent of their lovemaking, still felt the buzz from it. She doubted anyone else who knew the CFO of the prestigious Kansas City firm Landwehr Investments would guess he had such a wild side. Out of his business "uniform" he became the unrestrained lover she'd fallen in love with almost six years ago. He'd been extremely uninhibited this morning, more dominating and aggressive than he'd been in months. Not that she was complaining. She'd loved having his undivided attention, but she'd be pleasantly sore today.

"Don't you have a board meeting this morning?" His brown-eyed gaze met hers in the cheval mirror in front of him. Gone was the husky tone he'd used to growl naughty words to her a short while ago. Back was the tone of a man used to having his every word obeyed at his office…and in their marriage.

Obedience to someone else still came hard to her. While his life centered around constant meetings, many of them board meetings, she merely tolerated them. She preferred to be in the trenches as a volunteer working face-to-face with people. Because of his status in the community, Grayson thought it best for her to be involved in the organizational, the supervisorial part of worthy nonprofits. "I'll be there in plenty of time." She stretched like a contented cat and enjoyed the pull of tender spots from her well-loved body. "I'm enjoying lazing about here for now. Besides, you wore me out. I've really missed that."

Rather than responding to the way she'd stroked his ego, he turned to give her a disapproving look. "You've been doing a lot of 'lazing about' recently."

She fought against sending a disapproving look right back. Sometimes he was impossible to please. Here she was lying naked in bed, trying to give him a seductive pose, and all he could think about was how she didn't rush out of the house in the mornings like he did. She knew him well enough to know his definition of "lazing about" meant not being busy forty or more hours a week

—fifty, if you used him for an example. She couldn't be him, couldn't live by his code of work, work, and work some more.

"Really? You want to get into this sore subject now? After we just had amazing sex? Or maybe it was only me that felt that way." Her high from the experience was fast disappearing. She felt inadequate. Something that she'd been feeling more and more these last few months.

His brow furrowed in annoyance and there was something in his eyes that she couldn't quite read. She sensed something else was bothering him. Usually he just spit whatever it was out. He wasn't a man who minced words.

"No response to what I said?"

For a second he looked ready to snap at her, but then he shook his head. "I don't have time to argue with you." He went to the triple dresser and gathered up his wallet and watch.

You don't have time for arguing with me! Time, time, time. Everything with you is about blessed time! She pursed her lips in disgust behind his back. She wasn't a strict schedule kind of person, preferred to be more flexible about when she did things. She didn't even wear a watch and hadn't owned one in years. Yet he expected her to live his way, ruled by the clock. His way also included spending every waking minute doing things she hated, like going to board meetings. Not that the groups she worked with weren't worthy organizations. They just weren't her choices. She would have preferred to be involved with the United Way or Senior Services because of her social work degree and the work she'd done before marrying Grayson. So much of her life had changed when she'd decided it was more important to please her husband than do what she really wanted. But now she realized that decision had been wrong. She'd been putting off telling him though. She didn't want to let him down.

Heaving a disgruntled sigh, BJ sat up and leaned against the thickly padded headboard. She tugged the sheet over her, tucking it in beneath her armpits to cover her breasts. "I don't want to argue, either. I certainly don't want to take up too much of your precious time."

He turned to scowl at her. "You're being ridiculous."

"Am I?" She glared back at him. "This is the first time in weeks that you've bothered with more than a wham-bam moment with me. There's always some early morning meeting you're rushing off to. Or we're out at some society thing until late, and then we're both too tired to do more than fall into bed. Then the weekends… not much better, except you're off to the country club for golf unless there's a blizzard outside."

His handsomely carved face tensed; his shoulders stiffened. "Why didn't you tell me how you felt before now?"

The steam went out of her. It shocked her that she'd spouted out so many complaints. Sure, they had been building up inside her, but it wasn't like her to let her feelings out this way. She didn't usually find fault with others, which was another reason the boards she sat on now bothered her. Many of the society wives complained about everything from their lives to their husbands to their children. They complained subtly, but they complained. It made her uncomfortable. And she worried that she was becoming like them.

She sighed. "I understand your life and all that's required to maintain your position in the business community. Really I do. But my life is in transition at the moment and not completely by my choice."

He stuffed his wallet into the inner pocket of his suit jacket. "Are we back to my asking you to quit that part-time personal trainer position at the gym? It was for your own good."

"Insisting I quit," she corrected, knowing that was petty of her. "It was for your good more than mine. You used what happened as an excuse, because you wanted me to have even more time for stupid, boring board meetings."

Actually, it wasn't missing that particular job that was making her unhappy. She had approached the gym management about teaching exercise classes for seniors over sixty. They were hesitant, then she'd had the injury, and then he'd made her cancel their membership there.

His shoulders stiffened and she regretted sounding so sharp. She was just so frustrated.

"Those are important boards for you to be on." His tone was brittle, testy.

"Because they help your image. Yes, I know." She sighed. They weren't getting anywhere. They needed to sit down and seriously talk about this, except he never had the time. And she wasn't sure how to approach him about what she really wanted to do. She had a plan and was already working on it in secret, which would probably bite her in the butt eventually. Or get her butt warmed for going behind his back.

If he were easier to talk to…

Frustration with all of it made her antsy. She needed to get to the Y and work out an extra hour maybe. Lately she couldn't miss a day there without feeling anxious. But the Y membership was yet another problem she had, another secret she was keeping from Grayson. She needed to exercise.

His glance shifted to the bedside clock and back to her.

Impatience flashed in his eyes. "We've talked about this many times, Belinda Jo. You knew when we married that I expected you to perform in the community at the level required of my position. You agreed."

She held onto her patience, silently counted to ten, then twenty. "Yes, I knew you wanted a supportive wife and I thought I could live with it. And I am supportive. But…"

He looked at the clock again, clearly impatient to leave.

His attitude rubbed her wrong. She said bluntly, "But sitting on your choice of boards isn't fulfilling to me. I'm bored with them and I don't fit in with those women."

"Of course you do," he countered, jangling his keys.

"No, I don't!" At her snappish tone, he scowled. She fisted her hands, irritation driving her. "I'm not comfortable with them. Besides that, I'm tired of being your arm candy at society events."

"Arm candy?" He raised an eyebrow.

Of everything she'd said that was what he picked up on?

"The elegantly dressed woman on your arm that you lead about and show off. I'm more than that, dammit!"

"You're in a mood this morning and not a good one. When you've calmed down, we'll talk reasonably." He seemed to think about something, then he narrowed his gaze. "I heard that you've been skipping meetings, coming up with excuses."

She blinked. Someone had tattled on her? Why wasn't she surprised? Still, the idea was irritating. "You heard?"

A vein pulsed in the side of his neck. "Yes, one of my friends mentioned it at lunch yesterday. He heard about it from his wife. What have you been up to, Belinda Jo?"

She froze. "Up to?"

He didn't repeat himself, simply looked at her.

"I'm not sure what you're talking about." This was not the right time for discussing any of this. He was in a hurry. She was growing restless. She needed to exercise to get rid of the antsy feeling spreading through her.

She straightened the sheet over her lap. "I've only missed a couple of meetings." She needed to resign from those boards, but not until she talked this out with Grayson. He wouldn't be pleased. He believed in standing behind your commitments. She used to.... Her stomach squeezed with nerves. Letting him down would be difficult. But she was letting herself down by doing these things that didn't matter to her.

"Belinda Jo," he prodded, pulling her from her thoughts. "Is there something you need to tell me?"

Yes, but not now. "Don't you need to get going?" She tried an evasive maneuver. "I thought you had an early meeting."

His jaw tightened for a second. "You know I don't like secrets. It's easy to see that something is going on with you, that something is making you moody." He blew out a breath and jangled his keys again. "You've been disagreeable for a week now, maybe more. I think we need to work through this tonight."

"I don't want to 'work through' anything." That was never a pleasant experience. Yes, she was keeping a secret, about the

Y. She didn't like going against him and when she did, she paid the price by suffering a very sore bottom. But this was a complicated secret.

She fidgeted with the sheet and felt him watching her, waiting for her to say more. She wouldn't have this particular problem if she hadn't suffered a severe muscle strain a couple of months ago. Her doctor had warned her about doing too much exercise, advised her to cut back. Unfortunately, Grayson had come rushing into the emergency room after the stupid receptionist had called him. He'd walked into the examination room just as the doctor was laying down the law. Grayson had gone a step further. He'd insisted she stop the personal trainer job and drop their gym membership. She was only supposed to do limited working out on their home exercise equipment. It wasn't enough, though. She needed to have others working out around her. Afraid he'd find out if she went back to their former gym, she'd decided to join the Y instead. She liked it there and now she was pursuing plans to start a couple of classes for senior adults there.

"Belinda Jo."

She really hated the steady way he was looking at her. But she couldn't spill the Y thing yet. Joining behind his back to exercise would upset him. She understood he was worried about her, and she knew he would be angry and disappointed in her when he found out. He'd let her explain her reasoning, but there would still be a very unpleasant session over his knee for her deception. Still, she wanted her plan solidified before she presented all of it to him. The management was dealing with getting approval and then figuring out how to advertise it. It was all taking too long, which frustrated her even more. She needed to go exercise, to burn off the tension.

A glance at him told her she needed to say something. "For the most part, I do whatever you ask of me. I quit my job. I serve on a half dozen community boards that I hate. I'm all sweet smiles and the perfect hostess when you need me to be."

When she saw his frown deepen, she knew she should not have been so snappish. It was the frustration.

"What is wrong with you?" He narrowed his gaze as if to study her, as if he could determine the problem without her telling him what bothered her.

Wanting to distract him, she latched onto the first excuse that came to mind. "Headache." To support the idea, she reached up to rub her forehead.

His raised eyebrow implied he wasn't satisfied with her reason. Still, his gaze softened in concern. "Do you want me to get you an aspirin?"

Guilt weighed on her. "I'll get something in a few minutes." She gave a weak smile. "About tonight…we don't need to waste your time with…" She didn't want to say "with a spanking." She didn't want to put the thought of a spanking in his mind, although it was probably too late for that. Part of why she wanted to avoid a "discussion" was she well knew how grouchy and short she'd been lately. All the secrets led to stress and with it her attitude was getting worse with each passing day.

He walked toward her, looking for a second like the man who had made such hot, steamy love to her only moments ago. His nostrils flared and he leaned down to give her a good-bye kiss, as he always did no matter what they might be in disagreement about at the time

She breathed a sigh of relief and accepted the kiss, returned it, too. But she was pretty sure the problem of the moment wasn't solved.

He proved her right. When he straightened, his expression was dismal. "Taking care of your needs is never a waste of my time. We will, of course, discuss the situation first."

"Of course," she said in resignation. His decision to discipline her had already been made. He'd had enough of her attitude of late. So had she.

He strode across the large bedroom and then glanced back at her. "Depending on the severity of the spanking necessary, you may want to adjust your schedule tomorrow."

Her heart raced as he left the room. The severity of the spanking? Not good. Right now he was only disgusted that she'd skipped some meetings with flimsy excuses and the suspicion she was keeping something from him.

They had agreed long ago not to keep secrets. She understood that he expected her to suffer the consequences of breaking a trust. She didn't want a spanking, but she respected and loved him. If—when—he found out about the exercise thing, that she was going behind his back and against the doctor's recommendation, he would definitely not be happy with her.

When she finally got approval for her class at the Y and told him, he would be irritated because she'd gone behind his back. She would probably get spanked for that as well. But she would make him see the good she would be doing and how much it meant to her. He would fuss and fume a bit, yet she was pretty sure he would be proud of her in the end. At least, she hoped so.

If only the Y's management would make a final decision.

Her stomach knotted. Get to the gym. She could deal with anything after a good workout.

* * * *

Grayson sat in his Lexus in the garage for several minutes before starting the engine. He had an impossible day ahead, back-to-back meetings from nine o'clock until six. Already he was tired. He didn't like fighting with BJ, or knowing that she was unhappy. Worse was the feeling that he didn't know what was going on with her.

He'd learned yesterday that she'd skipped out on an important board meeting. She'd been supposed to report on a committee she headed, but she'd given the president an excuse about another conflict. She'd lied to the woman.

He'd seen BJ's calendar and there hadn't been anything other than the library board meeting on it. He should have asked her about the problem last night, but they'd had a business dinner to attend that went until almost midnight.

He punched the remote to raise the garage door and noticed the dark gray clouds, as gloomy looking as his thoughts. The matter with BJ had stayed in his mind all night. He'd slept restlessly, awakened on edge…and randy. Having gone without the intense kind of sex they both liked—as she'd said—for too long, he hadn't been able to resist going all animal with her.

He shifted uncomfortably, still semi-hard. He'd been in full dominant mode and she'd let him be as wild as he'd wanted. Yet even as he'd pounded into her, in the back of his mind, he'd known he needed to confront her. But what had he first talked about? Her attending a board meeting today, her lazing about. He'd known those were sore subjects.

Was he being unfair to her by choosing boards for her to be on? He'd thought she would like the library board and the board of the country club they belonged to in particular. When they had first married, she had mentioned that she wanted to be involved with the United Way and Senior Services. But after he'd strongly suggested some other organizations, she'd dropped the subject. Now he felt guilty for not seeing how much they had meant to her. As she'd just told him, she was more than a pretty woman to be led around by him. But he liked showing her off. He liked how she always spoke kindly to the many strangers she met. She didn't put on airs like so many of the other women he knew. She really listened to the people she talked with.

Clearly he was the one with a listening problem. Although she hadn't spoken about being unhappy until today, no doubt there had been signs he should have picked up on. He would have to pay better attention in the future.

When she'd laid into him about how he'd been neglecting her, it had hit him hard, especially now that he realized she was right. His business was important to him. But she was more important. She was the woman he loved and didn't want to ever live without.

Backing out of the garage, he felt frustrated. He'd rather be having a conversation with BJ right now than putting it off and trying to focus on the day's worth of meetings ahead. Their discussion wasn't going to be enjoyable. She was lying to other people; he'd bet she was lying to him as well. It hurt. He had thought they had a better relationship than that.

Didn't she know how much he cared about her? He'd listened to the doctor warning her to stop working out so much at the gym after she'd gotten injured. When she'd balked at the idea, he'd gotten worried. Then when she'd protested staying away from the gym because of her personal training obligations, he'd felt he had to step in and take charge of the situation. He'd told her to quit the job because it would only have kept her too close to the temptation of working out on all of that equipment. When she'd again protested, he'd taken a firmer stand and insisted they give up their membership to the gym. He'd seen it as protecting her, keeping her safe.

He'd hoped taking a more active part on the various boards would fill the slack in her days, help her get over quitting the part-time job. He'd been wrong.

Obviously that little job had meant more to her than he'd thought. He didn't mean to control her, to squash her ideas, to make her see everything the way he saw it. Her independence and self-confidence had been part of what had attracted him when they'd met at a fund raiser for Senior Services, where she'd been on staff as a new social worker. But she'd given up that job, had never really talked about it since then…other than occasionally mentioning that she'd like to do more with them. She'd talked once about wanting to help deliver meals to seniors. He'd vetoed the idea because he knew that some of the areas where the volunteers went were in unsafe parts of town. He wanted to protect her. Was she still unhappy about his decision?

Now that he thought about it, she didn't talk to him about much of anything beyond what he talked about concerning this party they needed to attend or that event he thought she should help with. Yes, it was long past time that they spent some serious time together working through these issues and what was making her so unhappy.

BJ was keeping something from him and it was wearing on her to keep the secret. Her attitude had changed drastically over the last month or so. She was still friendly when they went to the necessary social functions, but she'd been growing quieter around him when they were alone. He'd been so focused on work issues and so tired that he'd not given her change in behavior enough notice.

They had agreed on certain household rules before they'd gotten married. They would respect each other, support each other. They would share their lives and not keep secrets from one another. Plus they'd added a couple of special items to "their rules," helping her break some bad habits she struggled with from time to time. The worst of those were her occasional binges on chocolate when she was down about something or getting stuck in a cycle of staying up too late night after night to marathon watch movies.

It had been a while since he'd caught her bingeing on chocolate or dealt with her crankiness from the exhaustion of too many late nights. But she'd started pulling away from him, which he didn't understand. Plus he knew she had lied to the board president, and he had a feeling that wasn't the only time she'd lied lately. The whole lying matter needed to be dealt with immediately, firmly. There would definitely be a spanking tonight.

He wanted to know exactly what she was keeping from him. If she wouldn't come clean, he would give her some serious incentive. He didn't want to, but he might need to pull out the well-worn paddle. Neither of them liked that.

* * * *

"Are you okay?" Beth asked as she glanced at BJ from the elliptical next to her.

BJ patted her sweat-covered forehead with a hand towel. No, she wasn't okay. She'd been worried ever since Grayson had left the bedroom. She worried that more was going wrong in their marriage than her frustration and their lack of communication. It had been a while since he'd complimented her on something she wore, on how she looked, or the role she took with the community events.

"BJ?"

She smiled reassuringly. "Sorry, just catching my breath for a second there."

She swiped at the perspiration again. Her lungs burned; her thighs felt tight. Maybe she'd pushed it too much on the elliptical this morning. "I'm a little frustrated right now. All the delays in starting my classes.

The people I've mentioned it to keep asking about it, but I can't give them a definite start date." She sighed. "It's just so…so frustrating."

Beth stood still, catching her breath. "I have a feeling it's more than the classes. You seem unhappy." She looked concerned. "Are you and Grayson having problems?"

Were they? Yes… and no. "Not really, at least I hope we aren't." She worried her lower lip for a second. "He's losing patience with me, with my moodiness at home. Not that I blame him." But she knew there were reasons for her moodiness: the stress from wanting to start the classes, the knowledge that she'd gone against their agreement by keeping secrets, and her desire to resign from every one of the boards she sat on but refusing to do so until she talked to Grayson. Plus there was the whole issue of never having the time to talk to him.

Until tonight. But she wasn't ready for a talk tonight. There was no change yet on the class situation, and she didn't want to discuss anything to do with the Y without that being settled. Probably she was being silly about wanting it finalized before talking to him about it. Maybe it was because she'd let him convince her to quit the personal trainer job when she hadn't really thought it necessary. Maybe she believed she'd let him convince her to give up on this idea, too. She didn't want to take that chance.

"When was the last time you two went away together? Like Hawaii or even Las Vegas? Or a cruise?" Beth stepped off the elliptical. "Too long, in my totally biased opinion. Grayson is always so busy, barely pays you any attention. At least that's what you tell me." She stretched to her full five-foot-two inches. "Do you want me to have a talk with him?"

BJ laughed at the image of her petite friend taking on the almighty Grayson Landwehr, who would tower over her by a foot. Beth was an artist, free-spirited and not afraid to speak her mind about anything and everything. And Beth was fiercely loyal to her. For some reason Beth's lion-like protectiveness lightened her mood.

"I appreciate the offer, but I can handle him." She thought about Beth's comment. It was true that they hadn't gone on vacation in a couple of years. They hadn't even sneaked away for a romantic weekend. Most of their going out together involved being with other people, networking nights.

The almost faded memory of their heated time in bed this morning flashed into her thoughts. She had missed such passionate moments.

She was pretty sure he had, too. So much in their lives had changed over the last year, especially since the last merger. It was more than his being busier, having even more responsibilities. She couldn't quite figure out what the problem was, but he didn't share his business life with her anymore. She used to feel like they were a team. Now she felt alone. Superfluous. He didn't need her, except as arm candy, like she'd told him. The thought depressed her.

She started working the elliptical again. Pushing herself. Focusing on the way her thigh muscles protested, feeling the burn, allowing it to divert her from the lonely, sad feeling that had settled in her chest.

"How can you possibly do more?" Beth gaped at her. "Every muscle in my body is screaming, and you've been doing this easily twice as long as I have today."

BJ's body was screaming, too. But she couldn't stop. If she did, she would feel the pain of her life with Grayson falling apart. She'd skipped another meeting this morning to attend the Zumba class. She hadn't even let anyone know that she wouldn't be there. She felt guilty, irresponsible. Yet she just hadn't been able to make herself go. She definitely needed to find a way to tell him that she had to resign from the boards, even if she was letting him down.

She kicked it up a notch and now her calves tightened.

"I really think you should stop," Beth said, sounding distressed.

"I'm fine." Sweat rolled down the side of her face. She felt her ponytail lying limply on her shoulders. "Just another five minutes."

Beth looked hesitant and glanced toward the door. "I need to go, but I don't want to leave you alone."

"Really, I'm fine." BJ slowed her pace and smiled in reassurance. Beth had been the one to get help that disastrous day at the gym when she'd collapsed. She'd taken her to the emergency center, but she'd left when Grayson had shown up. She didn't know what the doctor had said or that Grayson had basically forbidden her to workout at the gym anymore. And she didn't know that Grayson didn't know she'd joined the Y.

Seeing the disbelief on Beth's face and the stubborn set to her chin, BJ sighed and eased the pedals to a stop. Grabbing the towel, she climbed off the elliptical. Her leg muscles felt like they were on fire. Probably jogging that mile and a half, followed by a half hour advanced Zumba class, and now almost forty minutes on the elliptical was too much. Tomorrow she would ease up a bit.

Beth started walking toward the doorway, clearly assuming BJ would be right behind her. But it took BJ a couple of seconds to actually convince her legs to move. Definitely she would work out a little less strenuously tomorrow.

Her stomach tensed. She had a showdown to face with Grayson tonight. Probably a bad one. *Depending on the severity of the spanking, you might want to adjust your schedule tomorrow.* Well, maybe she would be skipping a day or so here. She might even be standing a lot tomorrow after.... She shoved that unpleasant thought aside.

* * * *

Grayson hadn't been able to concentrate on business all day. He'd been terse with his staff. He had kept every meeting right to its schedule, not allowing a second longer for visiting. Finally he'd cancelled his five o'clock meeting and come home. BJ wasn't here yet, which had surprised him. As far as he'd known, she only had the one board meeting with the local botanical gardens today.

He finished changing from his suit into chinos and a casual shirt. He had a gut feeling that wherever she was it was what she'd been keeping from him. A secret. Maybe he should be worried that she was having an affair, but he wasn't. Maybe that was naïve of him. She was a passionate woman, usually full of spirit and life. Beautiful, too. One of the prettiest women he knew. She attracted men without even trying.

His hands fisted. He'd never seen her flirting with another man, and she'd had many opportunities during the numerous social events they attended. That didn't mean she hadn't been flirted with.

She loves you. His troubled conscience tried to get through his rare moment of doubting her. But did she love him as much as she once had? He wondered.

Where is she? He paced the bedroom, impatience thrumming through him. He wanted to talk to her, wanted to deal with this current issue, wanted to deal with any other matters that might come up in their discussion. His business life had taken all of his focus for months now. They'd let frustrations build up between them, and now they needed to face their problems.

He'd failed her in his duties as her head of household. In the past he'd handled her disciplinary needs either as they happened or at least once every month. It wasn't something he enjoyed, but they'd agreed to this kind of lifestyle. She expected to suffer consequences in certain situations. He'd let her down because he'd let other things take on more importance than his wife.

Dreading the discussion ahead and what might transpire, he went to the dresser. With a sigh, he pulled out the well-worn foot-long, wooden paddle in case it was needed. He hoped it wasn't. He carried it downstairs to his den, where they usually dealt with discipline. He never punished her in their bedroom. The bedroom was for making love or for making up, not for punishment.

He had just set the paddle on his large cherry wood desk when he heard the garage door opening. He tensed. He didn't look forward to another fight.

* * * *

BJ walked warily through the house, surprised at having found Grayson home so early. After showering at the Y, she'd decided to stop at the bookstore and then stopped for coffee at Starbucks. Okay, she'd avoided going home. She hadn't wanted to spend too much time there alone with her thoughts, with her apprehension about what would happen tonight.

"Grayson," she called out, nerves tangling in her stomach. "Where are you?"

She knew where he would be even before he answered. "In the den."

He didn't sound particularly angry, although she really couldn't judge his mood from the calmness in his tone. She shed her coat and lay it over the sofa in the living room on her way to see Grayson. It was hard to walk to the den anticipating a confrontation that wouldn't be pleasant.

She'd done a lot of thinking today, realizing that she couldn't keep carrying these secrets. With each day she kept them, she'd become more depressed, distanced herself more from Grayson. She didn't like who she'd become. And she didn't like hurting him or their trust in one another. It was time to come clean about her working out at the Y. She'd do her best to convince him the doctor had been wrong, that she was doing just fine. Still, she knew that she'd gone against Grayson's wishes. If she'd tried to talk it out with him instead of just ignoring his well-meaning command in the first place, she wouldn't be facing the consequences of going against him.

She stopped for a second to steady her nerves. More than coming clean about the Y and her exercising there, she needed to admit to him what she did and didn't like about her role in their life together.

Specifically she needed to tell him about her desire to resign from the boards she served on, at least most of them. There was one she did kind of like and would make more of an effort with in the future.

Buck up, you brought on this uncomfortable situation. You chose to go behind Grayson's back. You didn't trust in his love enough to open up with him. And that was what ate at her the most: that she'd not trusted him to get over his disappointment with her and support her decisions. She hadn't given him that chance.

She straightened her shoulders and stepped into the den's doorway. As she spotted her grim-faced husband sitting behind his desk, her courage to fess-up dimmed. It was more than his dour expression that had her eyes widening in dismay, her stomach roiling. It was the sight of her paddle on the desk.

"I guess this isn't going to be a good evening," she said quietly.

He didn't move, but his gaze held hers. "If you no longer agree to this arrangement, I'll understand."

She blinked at him. He was giving her an out, not that he didn't offer it each time. The offer settled her a little. All she had to do was take back the agreement that she'd given even before they married. If she did, he wouldn't spank her. She wouldn't ever go over his knee again, wouldn't feel his hard hand spanking her bare bottom. That horrible paddle would never blaze her bottom again. The belt he'd rarely thrashed her with would never touch her again. Not experiencing the paddle or the belt again strongly appealed to her. While she didn't enjoy the spankings either, she wasn't sure she wanted to completely cut out his disciplining her. Sometimes it actually helped her, although that was hard to explain. His caring for her even in such an embarrassing way... well, it was just another part of his loving her.

"Belinda Jo?" He was waiting for her decision.

"Are you falling out of love with me?" The words were out before she could stop them. It was something she'd feared as they'd been growing apart these last few months.

Pain and surprise flashed in his warm brown eyes. "I love you more than ever. It's because I love you that I'm offering you this choice. " He drew in a breath and she could see the strain of his frustration washing over his face. "I've been worried that I was losing you."

Tears misted her eyes and she walked toward him. She'd been such a fool. She stopped next to him, gently touched his face, let her thumbs stroke his five o'clock beard. "I've felt like you didn't need me anymore, other than for display. You don't share your day's ups and downs with me like you used to do. You…"

He swallowed hard and met her gaze. "I'm sorry, sweetheart." He pulled her between his legs, tugged her against him. "I was so wrapped up in my business that I missed the important things. I didn't see how dissatisfied you were with the community work. I failed to see how unhappy you were."

As he held her tightly, she rested her chin on his head. She felt his heart hammering next to her breasts. Hope filled her. "I shouldn't have let you ignore me. I should have made my desires and frustrations known, not tried to bury them."

Easing her back, he focused on her and she saw the depth of his feelings for her in his eyes. "Yes, you should have. I'm clearly a horrible mind reader."

She gave him a weak smile. "I'll do better from now on."

He nodded. "We both will do better. We'll get through this rough patch because I refuse to lose you. You are my first priority." He heaved a sigh. "I wanted to build up the business so you would be proud of me, so you would never have to worry about money. But I never intended for you feel like you took second place to it."

If only he'd said these things before… If only she'd told him sooner about how she felt…. They had a lot to work through, but their marriage was worth it.

"I've always been proud of you." Again she gently touched the side of his face. Familiar tingles of longing swept through her. She knew she could easily convince him to follow her upstairs and get him to show her a lot more of his sinfully wicked ways. But they could do that later…or tomorrow.

As strong as her desire to make love with him was, guilt kept her from acting on it. She was largely responsible for the rift between them and she wanted to take care of that. Right now she needed to prove to him just how much she loved him. They needed to have this discussion.

She stepped back, heart racing with determination. "I need to pay for having kept something from you."

He nodded and his brow furrowed. "What exactly have you been keeping secret?"

Her buttocks clenched as she anticipated the worst. He wasn't going to like her admission. "I've been going to the Y." He didn't need to know how many hours she spent exercising. And now that she thought about it, that was a lot of hours.

His nostrils flared. "Against my wishes. Against the doctor's recommendation."

She worried her lower lip a second. "It's my body. I know what I can handle," she said even though her leg muscles were still tingling after all she'd put them through today. "At least I think so."

"I forbid you from exercising at the gym because I was worried about you." He looked irritated, worried, too. "What do you mean by 'at least I think so'?"

Why had she let that slip? She tried to ignore his question. "When you did that, you were reacting to what happened on that particularly bad day. I admit, I overdid it then. I'm more careful now." Wasn't she? Or was she lying to herself ? There were days lately when her muscles hurt so bad that she didn't think she could even crawl out of bed. Yet she did. And then she went to work them harder by spending hours in class after class at the Y.

He frowned. "Are you? I've noticed you flinch a bit as you stand there. Were you at the Y today? Did you overdo it?" He blew out a deep breath. "You had a meeting today, but I have a feeling you didn't go. Am I right?"

She shifted nervously. Now he would be upset with her about both things, not telling him about exercising at the Y and about shirking her board duties. She was guilty on both counts. "They didn't really need me at the meeting. In truth, they don't need me at any of those meetings. And I'm not happy on that board." She raised her chin. "Actually I want to resign from that board and several of the others." There. She'd said it and the roof hadn't fallen in on her yet. The world hadn't exploded around her.

He studied her for several long seconds, a myriad of emotions playing in his eyes. Anger, then acceptance. Disappointment, then resignation. Finally concern.

"Belinda Jo, how often do you go to the Y? Don't lie to me." He didn't sound mad, as she'd expected, more worried.

His relative calmness surprised her. She hesitated, and then admitted, "Almost every day." Okay, she hadn't told him the whole truth. She'd been going every day for at least a little while.

His jaw tightened. "For how long each time?"

She avoided looking at him. "A few hours." She always went thinking she'd walk the track for only a mile or two, maybe do one of the classes, or spend an hour working on the weights. But then she'd end up being there several hours until she felt the stress she'd come there with replaced by physical exhaustion.

His frown deepened. "Classes? Weight equipment workouts? Swimming? What exactly?"

"A couple of classes. Weights, of course." She huffed, deciding not to tell him anymore. What did it matter? She hadn't injured herself again. "Why are you pressing me about this? I'm just exercising, just trying to maintain my figure, stay healthy."

"Your figure has always been perfect."

She blinked in delighted surprise at his statement.

But his next words took away some of her delight. "Actually, I think you're losing some of your former womanly softness, those gentle curves I like so much."

She bristled. "You don't like how I look now? Is that what you're saying?"

He shook his head. "I love you, but I'm honestly a little worried. I don't think what you're doing is healthy. A few hours of gym workout every day is excessive." He held her gaze, concern in his eyes. "I want you stop going every day. Limit it to a couple of times a week."

Her eyes widened. She panicked. "No! I have to go every day. I'll get fat. My muscles will—"

"You do not have to go every day," he said calmly, but firmly.

"Yes I do! It takes the edge off my frustration. I need it!" Her heart raced and the panic seemed to worsen.

He looked worried. "I think you have a problem, sweetheart." He sat up straighter.

A problem? "Just because I like to exercise—"

"No, because you can't seem to control the amount of exercise." He closed his eyes and then opened them and looked at her steadily. "Answer me honestly, BJ. Are you going to more and more classes? Skipping out on more meetings? Spending more and more time at the Y?"

It took her several seconds before she finally said quietly, "Yes. To all of it."

"Definitely a problem." He looked regretful. "I'm part of this problem, aren't I? My insisting you sit on boards that you apparently hate. My not paying enough attention."

Yes, he was a big part of her unhappiness. But so was she. She'd chosen not to stand up for herself, let him command what she did and didn't do. No, she was far more at fault in the problem. But he was acting like she was addicted to exercising or something. That was ridiculous! Wasn't it?

"I...I can't seem to be able to go a day away from the Y without feeling anxious. Missing a day of working out usually gives me a headache, makes me restless, makes me testy," she admitted quietly.

His expression was sad as he said, "I'm so sorry that I was blinded to what has been happening with you. I'll help you get through this. I promise."

It warmed her to hear the depth of his concern for her in his voice. He was being strong for her. She needed to be equally as strong. She shook her head. "I got myself into this situation. I just... I don't know. Working out makes me feel better about myself." She sighed. "But after I stop...well, I kind of crash."

"Feel better about yourself ?" He drove a hand through his hair. "God, I should have seen how unhappy you've been. But I promise you, we will deal with this together. Whatever it takes, including supporting you on what you want to do."

She nodded, fighting tears. She should have talked to him long ago instead of closing down, tamping down on her dreams. Or working behind his back on one: her exercise classes for seniors. She understood now that he would support her on this idea. She should have trusted in him.

"We need to get back to why we're here." The words were difficult for her to say but necessary.

He was quiet for a long minute. "Yes, we do. We'll face the compulsive exercise issue later, maybe with help."

She could still say No, not go to bed with a sore bottom tonight, bruised pride. But there were worse things, like Grayson being forced to stop being the man he was...a man who believed in domestic discipline, in taking care of her when she misbehaved. "I'm ready."

He looked relieved. "I'm going to spank you for keeping a secret, for going against me. You understand that, right?"

"With the paddle?" She didn't like looking at the elephant in the room, at the paddle. It really was an awful thing.

He held her gaze. "What do you think?"

Oh geez. She hated when he made her help consider her recent misbehaviors or attitude issues. He was watching her, waiting, testing her. "I suppose my failing to stand up to my community commitments lately is bad."

"Lying to them about why you weren't going to be there," he corrected.

She felt her face heat. "Or not even telling them I wouldn't be there, like today."

That admission made him frown even more. "Paddle?" she asked warily.

"It's more memorable, gets the point across better."

She nodded. He clearly thought she needed something memorable. He was probably right, but... She trembled just at the idea.

"I've decided against using the paddle. You did wrong and need discipline for that. But I'm at fault too. I can see that now." He held her gaze and sadness mixed with love in his eyes.

Relief swept through her, although she knew he would still spank her. She gave him a wobbly smile of understanding.

He sat in his big chair and pushed it back to make room for her. "Instead of lowering your jeans and panties you will remove them."

With her muscles so sore, it was difficult to contort around and remove them, but she did. She placed her clothing and her shoes on the leather sofa across the room. Face heating and struggling to look at him, she walked to him and assumed the position as expected, giving a soft moan when her stiff muscles protested. Her stomach brushed the soft fabric of his slacks. Her mound rested on his right thigh and, unable to stop the reaction, she felt moisture from arousal beading between her legs.

"Very good." He shifted her T-shirt high on her back, completely baring her bottom. Then he began what he called a "proper warm up." He spanked her cheeks steadily, starting off lightly, and slowly increasing the intensity.

She lie as still as possible, barely breathing, concentrating on getting through this first part without disgracing herself. She'd earned this over two months, and now she just wanted it done and behind them.

He spread her legs further apart and continued right on spanking one cheek and then the other. Since she wasn't experiencing real pain at this point, her body was confused. It responded to being close to her husband, to his scent, to desire. To not have control of her body and know that he must be seeing the moisture in her private place was a bit humiliating.

And then he sighed deeply and stopped the pre-spanking. She dreaded what he would say and what would happen next. But she didn't move until he gave her the instructions for the more serious part of the spanking.

"You will bend over the desk, bottom thrust out, legs spread apart shoulder-width." He helped her to her feet.

"Yes, Sir." Her bottom was warm, had a light sting to it. Soon it would be much worse. She tried not to think about that as she walked around the desk and moved into the position he desired. She bit back a groan at the pain of moving. She'd overdone it today at the gym, which was making all of this worse.

She tensed as he stepped around to join her. "I'm ready, Sir. Please give me the spanking I've earned." Every time she had to ask for her punishment the words were hard to say. But it was part of the ritual and the familiarity of it was oddly comforting.

He held his hand against her tingling bare bottom. "This will be a hard spanking. I don't tolerate lies, which you did by keeping this exercise matter from me. Understood?"

She hated dragging this out, but, again, his warnings were part of the discipline ritual. She curled her fingers around the opposite edge of the desk and got as ready as she could. "Yes, Sir."

Without another word he raised his hand and brought it swiftly down. Even prepared for it, she cried out at the first loud swat.

He gave her a second to gain control and then he began to seriously spank her. The swats came down rhythmically, powerfully. He gave her no breaks to recuperate between strokes. It wouldn't have mattered. She couldn't catch her breath, couldn't think of anything but the searing pain. She tried to lie still, but all too soon she had no control. She kicked her legs, struggled, wriggled. She sobbed out her misery and begged incoherently for it to end.

On and on it went. She had no idea how many swats she'd received. It didn't matter. "Please! Ohmigod! Please stop!" she finally screamed.

But her discipline only ended on his terms. The awful hard hand slammed down on her blazing bottom another three times.

He moved away. "You will stay there while I go put the paddle away."

The unused paddle. Thank God. Still sobbing, she heard him leave the room. She collapsed on the solid desk top. Oh she hurt. He hadn't spanked her this hard in a long time, and she certainly didn't want to experience it again anytime soon… if ever. No doubt his hand hurt as well.

She started to ease up and remembered his command to stay in position. She wanted to reach back and rub at the horrible sting, but didn't.

She thought about how he'd finally gotten back into his role of disciplinarian… It wasn't easy being a submissive wife. But she loved him, even that part of him. She was on familiar ground again.

"Would you like some cream applied?"

BJ jerked at Grayson's sudden return. She knew he was standing behind her, probably studying his handiwork. He'd once told her he didn't like having to spank her, but he did enjoy the sight of her red bottom. It had to be really red now.

Instead of responding to the cream question, she said, "Red enough for you?"

He moved closer, putting a big hand on each of her tender buttocks. She winced and clenched her cheeks. "Hot enough too."

He gently squeezed and she arched away from him, hissing. "I'm in too much pain for playing around."

His hands fell away and she relaxed. "Can I get up now?"

"Yes." He carefully helped her up. As she winced again and finally reached back to cover her poor bottom, he said, "Tough session, huh?"

She kept her hands in place, dreading walking upstairs to bed. "It could have been worse. You could have used the paddle." She met his gaze. "I'm sorry. Really sorry. Especially for not talking to you about the exercise thing. Or telling you how I really felt about those boards."

His eyes had grown warm and she noticed his erection pushing at the front of his slacks. But he drew in a breath and released it heavily. "You've paid the price for it. And we're going to deal with your problem together, just as I said earlier." He reached for her, held her to him. "I want you so damn bad right now. But I won't cause you more pain. Go on to bed."

Again she thought about having to climb all of those stairs. He was right, though, she might desire him, but now was not the time to indulge in another wild round of lovemaking. She headed for the door, looking back. "We're going to be okay now, aren't we?"

"Yes, we are." He spoke with such determination, such confidence. "I won't lose you, sweetheart. I can't."

She smiled at him in spite of all the issues they still had to work out, in spite of the fact that he'd just spanked her. "I can't lose you either."

She started to turn away and then decided to trust him with her other sort-of secret. If he chose to spank her for keeping it from him… well, she'd just as soon get that over with now, too. "There is something else, Grayson."

His shoulders slumped. "Another secret?"

Her buttocks pulsed from the pain of the spanking, but she forged ahead. "Not really. It's just something I didn't want to talk to you about until everything was set. I wanted you to be proud of me for working this all out on my own."

"I am proud of you," he said cautiously. "You don't have to earn that."

He didn't look angry, just a bit disappointed. Comforted by that, she said, "I'm hoping to start teaching a couple of exercise classes for senior adults over sixty at the Y. They're still trying to get all of the details finalized. But it's something I felt was needed there. It's something I can do and will enjoy." Did he hear the eagerness in her voice?

"You've missed working with seniors since you quit Senior Services. You've hinted at it, but I just didn't quite get it. I'm sorry." He smiled, a smile that spread across his handsome face and reached his warm eyes. "I'll support you in this however I can."

Tears slipped down her cheeks and she hurried back to him. As his arms wrapped around her, she sniffled. "I love you so much." She stepped back and repeated the words. "I love you."

This time instead of letting her go, he scooped her up. She hissed at the stinging pain, but shoved that aside. Whatever he had planned next was exactly what would heal them both.

THE END